MTV's THE REAL WORLD™ HAWAII

TRUE Confessions

by Alison Pollet

POCKET BOOKS

MTV books

NEW YORK   LONDON   TORONTO   SIDNEY   SINGAPORE

Special thanks to:

Jorge Alves, Jr., Amaya, Avideh Bashirrad, Atsumi, Becky, Brian Blatz, Eduardo A. Braniff, Liz Brooks, Mary-Ellis Bunim, Avery Cobern, Colin, Tricia Connolly, Judith Curr, David, Tod Dahlke, Twisne Fan, Lisa Feuer, Scott Freeman, Erin Galligan, Dawn Garcia, Mike Glazer, Kristen Harris, Russell Heldt, Greer Kessel Hendricks, Janet, Lauralee Jarvis, Jason, Justin, Kaia, Jeff Keirns, Teri Kennedy, Kate Keough, Leif Knyper, Matt Kunitz, Andrea LaBate, Suzanne Leichter, Lindsay, Calvin Maeda, Jimmy Malecki, Malo, Matt, Michelle Millard, Laura Murphy, Jonathan Murray, Nathan, Neil, Donna O'Neill, Ed Paparo, Mark Raudonis, Rebecca, Ruthie, Sara, James Sartain, Charlotte Sheedy, Lisa Silfen, Robin Silverman, Donald Silvey, Dave Stanke, Jonathan Singer, Jerome Singletary, Liate Stehlik, Peter Szymanski, Stephen, Julie Taylor, Teck, Van Toffler, Theresa Velz-Ortiz, Kara Welsh.

Book design by EPHEMERA INC.

An original publication of MTV BOOKS/POCKET BOOKS

POCKET BOOKS, a division of SIMON & SCHUSTER INC.
1230 Avenue of the Americas, New York, NY 10020

ISBN: 0-671-03701-3

First MTV Books/Pocket Books trade paperback printing, November 1999

10 9 8 7 6 5 4 3 2 1

All the cameras, film, and processing for the cast and crew are courtesy of FUJI.

Photo Credits:

Jimmy Malecki: front and back cover; pages 6, 8, 9, 10, 11, 12, 13, 14, 15, 16, 17, 18, 19, 20, 21, 22, 23, 24, 25, 27, 28, 29, 30, 31, 32, 34 , 35, 36, 38, 41, 42, 43, 44, 51, 52, 68, 70, 71, 72, 80, 84, 85, 88, 89, 90, 91, 93, 94, 98, 99, 100, 101, 102, 103, 106, 107, 108, 109, 110, 112, 113, 114, 115, 116, 118, 119, 120, 122, 123, 124, 125, 126, 128, 132, 133, 134, 135, 136, 138, 139, 140, 141, 142, 143, 144, 145, 146, 147, 148, 150

Dimitri Halkidis/MTV: page 4

Amaya: pages 7, 33, 37, 47, 65, 71, 81, 82, 90

Teck: pages 7, 40, 49, 50, 56, 64, 66, 75, 88

Colin: pages 7, 26, 27, 39, 41, 45, 46, 49, 64, 65, 75, 77, 79, 83, 86, 92

Matt: pages 7, 36, 38, 40, 41, 42, 55, 56, 58, 61, 62, 66, 67, 72, 74, 75, 76, 77, 90, 92

Mark Raudonis: pages 7, 72, 82

Kaia: pages 11, 31, 60, 64, 67, 73, 86

Ruthie: pages 39, 53, 78, 90

Michelle Millard: page 65

Kenny Hull: pages 97, 131

Jennifer Emil: pages 96, 97, 98

Matt Kunitz: pages 70, 125

Janet: pages 124, 127, 129, 143

Lindsay: pages 124, 125, 129, 149, 151

Stephen: pages 124, 125, 145, 150

Nathan: pages 125, 134, 137, 138, 139

Rebecca: page 125

Courtesy *Honolulu Star-Bulletin*: page 73

Courtesy *Playboy*: page 152

Billy Rainey: pages 130, 153

THE CONTENTS

THE FOREWORD

In this little foreword, I will be answering some popular questions and revealing some of the greater insights from my show, the timeless classic *The Real World–New York*. In case you are wondering who I am: I am Becky. Yes, you read it right: Becky. That wouldn't be Julie, the pretty, smart, and quirky Southerner. And it wouldn't be that witty and bodacious African-American, Heather. I am Becky. I was Becky. I will forever be Becky. The grouchy one with that certain *je ne sais quoi* about her hairdo. Remember me now? I knew you would.

Now, I'm sorry to say it, but you all know that there will be never be a cast as special as the New York cast. I hate to boast, but we were truly original. No one was like us. We are the Native *Real World*–ers. The Indigenous *Real World*–ers. The Best. Don't get angry. What do you expect? It wasn't like any of us ever said: "Hey look at *that* show, man! I wanna be on that!" like the rest of you suckers. (Relax, it's called a joke....) We were the first ones for the series. We had no clue what we were doing. And yes, folks, we survived.

That said, we can move on to some handy tips to see you through the next few years.

I. I have two words for you brave new *Real World*–ers: don't panic. Your notoriety will bring some great things, but since you're famous for, well, being fabulous you, it will also bring on some more dodgy scenarios. Like the following one:

A few years ago, I was at an outdoor auto show in Oregon behind a table helping out a friend sell some cool vintage parts. I was suddenly approached by a rather sticky, three-toothed young man in an MTV baseball hat and a heavy-metal band T-shirt who stared at me, drooling. "Hey aren't you Becky from *The Real World*?"

"That's me!" I replied, eyes darting in all directions and looking madly for an exit sign.

"Can I ask you a question?"

"Yes, I suppose you may," said I, quickly preparing myself for the mind-numbing list of questions soon to come. This is part of the job, after all. I was expecting to hear:

1. Do you still stay in touch with your cast members? (Some of them.)

2. Do you really hate black people? (No, never did.)

3. Did you get married to Bill, the director? (Not that I am aware of.)

4. Did you shag Bill, the director? (Mmmmm, yes, a few times, thank you.)

5. Did Julie sleep with Eric? (I have no idea.)

6. Were you playing a character or are you really this much of an idiot? (Refuse to comment.)

I was prepared for any of those mind-numbing marbles, but what came out of the mouth of this star-struck, innocent boy's lips? It was: "What on earth are you doing HERE? You're rich. You're famous. You have a house in Bel Air with the Fresh Prince! Aren't you scared to walk around here without your bodyguards?"

Enough said, right?

Do you see what I am getting at here? You can admire the magic of television, but beware the logic of illusion! Dig the suspension of disbelief, but know that there will be strangers with weird ideas about your existence! If you are going to be a *Real World*–er, believe in your reality—but only sort of.

In the end, I did, of course, inform the young man that I was not in fact Becky, but her twin, set up as a decoy so she could pick out a good used car in privacy. He was very polite, and happy to be let in on the secret. Everything always works out for the best if you just stay calm.

II. *The Real World* only helps those who help themselves. *The Real World* is not about making anyone's career happen. If you didn't have a career to begin with, the likelihood is that you're not magically going to get one. And, say, if you are a gorgeous and talented yet latent genius, *The Real World* won't help you much with that, either. I learned that the hard way.

Seriously though, there are many *Real World* alumni who have wonderful careers. Look at Judd and Pam from the San Francisco cast. They are fabulous. That's because they worked hard when they were anonymous people and they work hard as not-so-anonymous people. The show didn't make their lives; they did. Same with me: I never worked hard before the bloody show and I don't work hard after the bloody show.

So, be who you are and stick to it. Have character and goodwill. Which brings me to my next topic: your "15 minutes of fame."

III. As you probably already know, you will be recognized. You will have a face known to many impetuous, alternative-music–blasting, hormonal, pierced, and tattooed strangers. And some kids will know you, too. As a result of your fame, there will be many secret doors opened to you for a short period of time. You will have people across the world writing you letters, wanting your advice and wanting you to shag them, again (key phrase here) for a short period of time. You will have a window of opportunity that few experience *for a short period of time.* You will have become Andy Warhol's 15-minute wet dream. This is where your ethics and values will come into play as a human being. What do you do with your minuscule moment of fame?

Hmmm, so many choices....Now, as we all know, fame is a whopping load of bullocks as far as personal development and self-respect go. But you can use fame for a good cause, or a good shag. It's up to you.

Judd, our centerfold for today, worked with the Pedro Zamora Foundation, using his influence quite effectively to raise awareness and funds for the AIDS epidemic. He was passionate and altruistic; he put others before himself. I think this is a marvelous example of character and goodwill. I, on the other hand, became a pseudo-radical and happily told the White House to piss off when they tried to recruit me for their "Stop Smoking America" campaign.

You choose.

IV. It's just television! Lighten up. The show will always be the same, but you will grow—no matter what you did to your roomies on the show. Don't bog yourself down with the mistakes you think you made. It's inevitable you'll act like a dork on at least one occasion. We will laugh with you—not at you. You have the power! And...

V. The end is just the beginning! Enjoy, but beware. Respect, but party freely. And just be you; like Mama always told you to be. Whether you are a fabulous flash in the pan, like moi or just an ordinary Joe. Relax and enjoy.

Good luck and see you all in the box.

—Becky

Becky, otherwise known as Rebecca Blasband, released her first original music CD, RAPT, on Mercury/Polygram in 1997 to rave reviews from a few family members and a small colony of mice in Northern Europe. She is currently residing among her people in Northern California, has changed her name to Elvis, and is working not very hard on a one-woman show titled:

TARGET: A Message of Peace

or

How I Cruised the Outer Limits of the Collective Unconscious through Every Rock Cliché Known to Man.

Look for it live sometime in the next millennium.

THE REAL WORD

didn't come to Hawaii to change the world. I came to talk to as many women as possible and eat as many pineapples as I could. And so I accomplished everything I wanted to. People may scoff at it, but I feel as though this is a launching pad for my career as an actor, producer, and filmmaker. I know superstardom hasn't happened for *Real Worlders* in the past. I don't care. I'm me, Teck Money Money. I'm gonna get it all done. And I'm gonna do it myself the Master P. way. Look, short and simple, I came to Hawaii to start my career. I've always felt like a star. I've always had a lot of confidence. And now I'm ready. It's like you gotta just know. You gotta just believe.

So, hell no, I never cried on *The Real World*.

homeboys and my family. My homeboys expect to see me macking on the ladies, and so I had to do it for them. I could've been even more off the wall, but, hey, my mom's gonna be watching too. Honestly, I couldn't wait to go home and watch the show with my homeboys. They're the realest people—my high school friends and college friends.

So, no, I wasn't going to Hawaii to stir it up. I'm twenty-three years old. For me, all that drama was: been there done that. In many ways, I felt like I had an advantage over my roommates. I've been on my own since I was eighteen. I've had five years to make my mistakes. I was past all that nonsense. Now, here's a funny thing. I felt old in the house. I really did. But at the same time, I felt like I was the

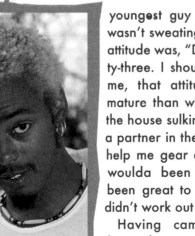

I FEEL LIKE I'M CHARLIE FROM WILLY WONKA AND THE CHOCOLATE FACTORY AND I JUST GOT THE GOLDEN TICKET. WHY WOULDN'T I FEEL THAT WAY? FOR ME, THE REAL WORLD WAS TECK PROMOTIONS 101, MY ENTRY INTO SHOW BUSINESS.

There was no reason for me to cry or even get depressed. And no, I never got my feelings hurt. It'd be hard to hurt my feelings, because I think I'm the man. Honestly, I was happy the whole time I was in the house. I don't know why any of the others cried or got upset. I hope they wouldn't cry to get attention. I mean, damn, I watched *The Real World* before I came on this show. I knew what it was about. I knew that people got upset and explored their emotions, but that wasn't going to be me. I had one goal: to let people know I was a star so that whenever I have a CD out, they buy it and whenever I have a movie out, they pay to see it. See, I had my mission, and I didn't sway from it.

I also came to Hawaii with an image, one I needed to protect and maintain—for myself, my

youngest guy in the sense that I wasn't sweating the small stuff. My attitude was, "Damn, I'm only twenty-three. I should be partying." To me, that attitude is a lot more mature than wanting to sit around the house sulking. I do wish I'd had a partner in the house, someone to help me gear everyone up. Ruthie woulda been cool. She woulda been great to roll with. But it just didn't work out that way.

Having cameras in my face changed me, yeah. The Teck and Tecumshea thing, it may sound like a line but it's true. When I'm at home chilling with my family, I'm the little Tecumshea they saw running around in his diapers when he was two. That's the calm, kick-back side of me. Then there's Teck, the social side of me. It's like Will Smith and The Fresh

Prince. I'm comfortable playing a lot of roles, and on *The Real World* I did just that. I was Mr. Crowd Hyper, Mr. Concerned Roommate, Mr. Smooth Operator. Yeah, sometimes I was acting. You can call it that. But should I feel bad? Like that wasn't *real*? I don't think so. What does one naturally do when there are two cameras in your face? You behave like you would, but you step it up a notch. At least that's what I do. Now, I'm not saying I ever did anything I wouldn't have done otherwise. Ninety-eight-point-five percent of my actions were how I would have acted without cameras. The rest was frosting on the cake.

As far as I see it, that's what I signed up for: to make things happen; to play the fool. And although I kept this to myself, I cared about ratings. I don't mind admitting it. I want people to watch the show. I want to entertain them. So, yeah, I thought about ratings when I went out to get my boogie on. And, yeah, I was happy when Ruthie gave her lap dances. And, yeah, I think Colin shoulda been touching Amaya's booty even more. I want people to see us. Does that make the experience less "real"? I don't think so. That's who I am.

I gave *The Real World* everything I wanted to give them. And I don't have a single regret.

The Real Word on... TeCK

AMAYA: Teck is fun. Having him there was like having a little bit of sunshine in the house. You never get too deep with him. That's very refreshing since other people in the house were always trying to be all Dorothy Parker. Teck's very caring in his own way. He knows what's going on, he just doesn't want to get too involved.

KAIA: I grew up with people similar to Teck. I grew up knowing men like him, *people* people, guys into the music scene. Teck was very focused on a side of himself that was excited and charismatic. He kept up a lot of energy and it was impressive. But there was another side of him. As his roommate, I saw it. I'd be waking up when he was getting home, and we'd have some good talks.

RUTHIE: There are certain people who think that being strong is not crying. Teck's one of those people. He doesn't realize that being strong means showing a lot of emotion. Courage and strength is not just being the man. You also have to be human.

COLIN: I enjoy Teck. I enjoy his behavior. In Teck's eyes, he's always been a star. He was one before he got on the show. He's light-hearted and fun. That doesn't mean I agree with everything he says. He can be sexist and sometimes I'm not party to that. He's also a BS-er in front of the camera and when it's not there he's up-front. He had an agenda and he got away with it.

JUSTIN: What I have to say about Teck is that I'm still waiting to really meet him.

MATT: It would be impossible not to like Teck because of his charisma. He never revealed anything about his personality that was unlikable. He's a fantastic guy to party with, but I can't see having a deep conversation with him. Our talents complement each other. I love to create, love to write. And Teck is a star. If he ever needs anything, I'll be there to help him. The two of us can get things done.

TECK: I'm closest to Kaia, and then Colin and Matt, and then the rest of 'em. I plan on keeping in touch with everyone, though.

from the CONTROL ROOM

Matt Kunitz, Supervising Producer: Teck has two sides to him: the great-time party guy and the wanna-be governor who can get the job done. When work needed to be taken seriously, he was up to the task. More than any of the other roommates, he took advantage of everything Hawaii had to offer.

Mary-Ellis Bunim, Creator: It's interesting that Matt (Kunitz) would mention Teck as the governor. This guy is walking charisma with a soul, with passion. If he channels that creative juice he will accomplish everything he will ever set out to do. Why stop at governor? Why not president?

Jon Murray, Creator: Teck is one of the most charismatic people we've come across in years. From what we observed and from what his friends have told us, the Teck we caught on camera is the same as the Teck off camera. Teck's whole life is one big performance.

The Real Word from...

amaya

feel like I went through some hard times in Hawaii, especially toward the end. So it's pretty surprising to me that I came out of the whole process feeling so good. Then again, I have nothing to be sad about. Except for the fact that maybe I'm too trusting. But, that doesn't matter, because even though I trusted people I shouldn't have, I'm coming away from the experience a lot stronger.

Kaia asked me if I considered anyone in the house a true friend. Friends take time. So, no I did-

Here's the thing: I didn't come to Hawaii to showboat and be a star. Teck is the biggest camera hog, but it's all out of fun. Matt and Kaia aren't camera hogs per se, but they definitely wanted to be seen in certain specific ways. Kaia wants to be known as the deep poet who can step away and observe. Myself, I don't feel this need to feign intensity. You know what happens when you act so seriously all the time? You get old. Quickly. You turn into Jack Kerouac or something. As for Matt, it's almost like he made it his duty to get involved

> STRAIGHT OUT, I'VE NEVER DEALT WITH SUCH TWISTED PEOPLE IN MY WHOLE LIFE. I FEEL SO MANIPULATED. I WAS THE VICTIM OF SOME VERY BORED PEOPLE. BY THE WAY, IF IT'S NOT ALREADY TOTALLY OBVIOUS, I'M TALKING ABOUT KAIA AND MATT.

n't have any true friends in the house. In fact, I can pretty much guarantee that there are three people in this house I'll never talk to again. Can I just say that I hate being so negative? Because seriously, overall, this experience was way more positive than negative. I really loved Hawaii. I got to live in a beautiful house with an amazing pool, which I snorkeled in. I got to look out at the ocean from the house and feel like it was mine. I got to go to India. I went skydiving. We had a great job with a wonderful

and giving boss. I had what you'd call a romance with someone I want to keep in touch with forever. But then there was all this deception. It's just really hard to see past it, to stay positive in the face of it.

Believe it or not, if I could do *The Real World* again, I would. It's just that I won't ever be able to trust people as easily. And that's sad.

in every situation. He even tried to get into Colin's and my relationship. I seriously question his motives.

But karma comes back to get you, if you know what I mean. Although I was called on it, I really don't question that I'm a good person. I know the crew thinks I am. And, really, in the end, they know a lot more about you than your roommates do. Consider how much more time they spend with you! The support I got from the crew during the last week of production was amazing. Obviously they couldn't advise me or talk to me at great length, but I could feel like they were standing by me. It was just subtle things. The way they said hello to me on the batphone, that kind of thing.

I was a *Real World* watcher, and I never knew how much work went into it. I saw every season except Miami. It's true what *Real World* producer

Matt Kunitz says: You have no idea what it's going to be like until you get there. I had no conception of how much filming they did. It truly is 24/7. Silly me, I thought there'd be breaks. Oh, and you know another unexpected thing? Because they reflect the light in a weird way, you can't wear white clothes on camera. That knocked out like half my wardrobe. One night, when the cameras were somewhere else and we were alone in the house, Colin and I rebelled and ran around the house in white clothes. It was an all-white party and it was fabulous.

I hope those are the kinds of times I think about when I remember *The Real World*. And I hope I remember how much growing I did. I came to Hawaii because I wanted a challenge and hey, I got a challenge. When I came to the house, I was bright-eyed and bushy-tailed. I was dying to meet all the people and have a lot of fun and just have this post-college little life before I moved on and entered the working world. And I got that—and a few life lessons too! I credit Ruthie for helping me find strength during the last moments. She knows it sucks to be the center of conversation, and she helped me see beyond the phoniness. "Don't trust anybody here," she told me. "I don't." She helped me see the light. For that reason, she has my total devotion.

I admit it: I left the show on some bad notes. But I'm strong enough not to let it bother me. I have the consolation that I gave people a chance. I tried to be a friend.

The Real Word on... AMaya

TECK: Amaya will be an excellent wife. She's very sweet and very naive. She's also a good actress. She can cry at the drop of a hat. One thing though: I don't know why she wore those beat-up shoes on the first day.

RUTHIE: I think Amaya has so much to be proud about. I don't know why she's so negative and moody. She can be cruel—well, not cruel, that's too harsh a word. But insensitive; she can definitely be that. When everyone started dissing on her in the end, I wasn't going to get petty about all of it. Amaya was rude to me and all that s**t, but who cares? I don't think she knows how she acts. When the roommates confronted her, the look on her face was just shock. She didn't even know she'd been rude. You get what you give.

MATT: I think Amaya's a talented and creative woman who will succeed as long as she believes in herself. But in my opinion she has serious self-esteem issues.

KAIA: Amaya is a wonderful person. I loved being around her. But she's very moody. She's the moodiest person I've ever met. She says she's different at home, and I'd like to see that. I do hope we become friends. It'll just take a while.

COLIN: Amaya's an intelligent, funny, and sensitive woman who has the tendency to take people for granted.

JUSTIN: What can I say about Amaya? Good luck! That about sums it up.

AMAYA: Colin, Ruthie, Teck, Matt, Justin, and, in last place, Kaia.

from the CONTROL ROOM

Matt Kunitz, Supervising Producer: If a cast member interacts with a crew member or vice versa, they're "line-crossing." If anyone from this cast wanted to "line-cross," it was Amaya. She "batphoned" probably five times a day. She looked for solace from the crew, and I'm afraid we just couldn't give it to her. Amaya had significant problems connecting with the roommates. And toward the end of her time in Hawaii, she made some unfortunate strategic mistakes. But I also think she grew a tremendous amount. The way she called Kaia out for shunning and betraying her? She would not have been able to do that six weeks earlier.

Mary-Ellis Bunim, Creator: I'm happy to say that I saw Amaya's potential to be a great cast member the moment I met her in San Francisco. She has such relatable issues: needing approval, poor body image, insecurity about the future. She works at being honest, yet has an innate dramatic streak. She'll be fascinating to watch as she evolves.

Jon Murray, Creator: Amaya can't help but be herself even in front of a camera. She didn't censor herself; to the contrary, she let us see it all: good, bad, and everything in between. As a result, I think she's grown a lot from the experience of being on *The Real World*.

COLIN

I n response to the accusation that *The Real World* isn't real, here's what I have to say: *The Real World* is like Disneyland; the extenuating circumstances in which you live are not real. However, the interpersonal relations among cast members are very real. For example, you might not normally ride roller coasters, just like most don't live in mansions on the beach. But if you break up with your girlfriend on a roller coaster, or fight with a roommate in the *Real World* house, those interactions are still real. As real as they can get in front of cameras.

Hawaii is just TV to me. I want to move on and put it behind me, internalize what I've learned. In my mind, the minute I left Hawaii, I wanted to stop analyzing what happened there. I don't get people who are still worried about what happened, who are still dwelling. Get over it. I'm past it. I'm glad to be back with my friends. I'm glad to be back with my family. I'm on the exact same career path I was on before. I'm the same guy I was before. I have no delusions of grandeur. I think I'm still the same average-looking guy who likes his friends and sports and hanging out. People who

PEOPLE WOULD JUST GO OFF ON MONOLOGUES ABOUT WHO THEY WERE AND WHERE THEY WERE FROM AND WHAT THEIR BACKGROUNDS WERE. I DIDN'T PARTICIPATE. I DON'T THINK ANYONE EVEN REALIZES I'M HALF PUERTO RICAN/SPANISH/HISPANIC. FOR ALL INTENTS AND PURPOSES, I'M JUST ANOTHER WHITE GUY.

For anybody in the future who's going to do *The Real World,* here's a tip: never go on this show with secrets. It's not worth your time, production's time, or the viewers' time to hide things. It's too difficult to censor yourself all the time, to hide things; it gets the better of you. I don't know how Teck did it. He was just incredibly selective with what he showed of himself. And Justin, I don't feel like he was very open either. I don't know why he was like that. He totally withdrew from work and the house, and in the end he left. He says it was for family reasons, and I sympathize with and believe him. I know other roommates will question the motives behind his departure, but I don't. I take him at his word. One thing I've learned from this process is that it's not worth my time and energy to analyze why other people say or do things.

At this point, everything that happened in

drop out of school and think they're going to attain some fame from this, *please.* My motto is, keep your ass in school unless you get some full-time offer. Like Kaia, she reapplied to Berkeley, but I'd be very surprised if she ended up back there.

Here's something: the best time I had in Hawaii was when my friends Trevor and Mike were there. Here's something else: I had more fun doing the casting special than the whole time in Hawaii. For me, the casting special was the best. Think about it: three best friends just BS-ing in front of the camera. What could be better? I heard someone say it wasn't fair that I was on the casting special, because I had a better sense of "the production side." Well, whether it was fair or not that I was on the casting special, I don't care. I don't think knowing what the other side was like affected me at all. I was more open than anybody who would say that.

I guess maybe it could be interpreted as unfair that I had some sense of who might be on the show, but it's not like I knew exactly who would make it. I could guess, though. I guessed all the guys right. But I guessed all the girls wrong. I was actually shocked to see Amaya and Kaia. Amaya, during our follow, was totally uncomfortable. I didn't think she was acting like herself in front of the cameras. So I was surprised to see her. And Kaia, I don't know, I just had a feeling she wasn't a strong candidate. Ruthie had come into casting late, so I'd never even met her.

There were a lot of things to deal with in Hawaii, things that were new for me—like being removed from my best friends and having a relationship with a roommate. I've learned a lot, living through the last four months. So, for many reasons, it'll be difficult to watch the show at certain points. I don't want to see Amaya and me fight. I don't think I'll want to see Ruthie in the grips of her drinking prob-

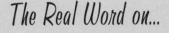 

MATT: I think of Colin as a true friend. We're buds. He's an honorable, stand-up guy. I just like him. I hope to be friends with him forever. Because of our geographical proximity to each other, he'll probably be my closest friend after leaving the show. We're up-front and honest with each other. He can talk your ear off about the roommates' negative aspects, but he can also get along with them. He's a schmoozer.

RUTHIE: Colin's a fun guy. He's the last person I'd expect to think was real. But on our trip to Hana, we just had fun. We didn't worry about petty stuff. He doesn't act older than he is. I appreciate that. Of the whole house, Colin and I had the best time together.

KAIA: I feel as though Colin was hesitant to approach me for a while. Mainly, I think that was because of my attachment to Justin. I'm sorry about that. In many ways, Colin and Justin are polar opposites in the way they approach things. I feel I was where they met in between. I didn't really appreciate Colin's humor when I first met him in casting. But I got into it later on. He's a friend who brought out my lighter side. That said, Colin can be so gross sometimes. He burps and farts freely and likes to talk about it. That bothered me.

JUSTIN: I have a lot of hope for Colin's good qualities. He's impassioned, but also emotionally frail. I find that very appealing. In retrospect, I think he got off easy in the house. He was really self-consciously guarded about his experience in the casting special. Aside from the fact that he's the straight white alpha male, I felt like he went on the show already having an edge. Doing the casting special gave him that edge. The entitlement rituals he danced during the show were deeply sketchy. All that aside, I still caught good glimpses of him. He's mostly fun.

TECK: Colin's a good-looking nerd. He's young. When his friends Mike and Trevor came into town, you could really tell that. He was carefree. I wouldn't say Colin grew up in Hawaii, but he did become more comfortable with his surroundings. He was a fish out of water who flopped around until he found the tide pools.

AMAYA: I'm going to miss Colin very much. And I hope that one day we can just be regular people and have a cup of coffee together. Actually, neither of us drink coffee, so hot chocolate. I care about Colin more than he knows. I hope he enjoys college, has a lot of fun, and finds love.

COLiN: I don't think I'm really close to anyone. If I had to rate them, Justin would be last. Kaia and Ruthie tie just above Justin. Teck next. Then Matt and Amaya.

from the CONTROL ROOM

Matt Kunitz, Supervising Producer: Colin is a bit of the fun boy next door. He's very humorous. And during our time in Hawaii, he was also open and honest. I think it was because he did the casting special that he was that way. He liked and trusted us, and had the benefit of knowing what production goes through. Yes, he's got a little bit of an attitude. I'd say he's incredibly stubborn, but then so am I. The two of us could really argue. I think he really enjoyed that.

Mary-Ellis Bunim, creator: Colin's a star. Will he be an actor? A sportscaster? Who knows? He's smart, funny, great-looking, and I think he'll be a fantastically successful person. Meanwhile, he's one of the most likable and relatable cast members we've ever had on the show.

Jon Murray, creator: Colin used the confessional to vent about his roommates, particularly when he thought they were being fake. If it weren't for the confessional, I think he would have exploded!

lem, even though I think it'll be good for her to see. I won't enjoy seeing myself cry if that even gets on. I'll never hear the end of that from my friends!

I would like to be seen as someone who is very funny and lighthearted, but also has a serious side. I don't know if viewers will get to see the sensitive side, but I hope they do. I also hope they'll see the parts of me that are messed up, not right, and not acceptable. Maybe they'll realize they're like that too and want to change.

RUTHIE

Before I left for *The Real World*, a friend's mom gave me a warning. She said, "Don't do anything you'll regret." She knows me pretty well—drinking and partying included—so when she said, "You can be wild, Ruthie," she knew what she was talking about. My friends, they were cheering me on. They were like, "Go crazy! It's 'Ruthie's World!'" One friend even predicted I'd get kicked off for partying too hard—although she thought it would happen on the second week.

At college I do crazy stuff. I pissed in a frat-house keg, when some of the guys were messing with my sisters. I had a fight—a fistfight, actually—with a group of girls. I ended with scratches, but one of them actually had a dislocated shoulder. I

seen? Teck told us he had an agenda. For him, it was to be known as the ladies' man. I panicked. I was like, "I don't have an agenda. I never even thought about how I'd be perceived." Justin said he didn't care how people saw him, he was on vacation. He was in Hawaii to have a good time. Matt said something like, "As long as people know about my writing talents, I'll be happy."

I guess you could say we were getting paranoid. It was still the honeymoon period, but we were getting nervous. Like, "Whoa, what are we going to look like?" I remember Teck saying he didn't mind playing "the token black guy." I was thinking: *why would you want to be that?* Even though viewers may end up stereotyping you, you can't play into it. Was I supposed to play the local Hawaiian girl?

FOR THE FIRST TIME IN MY LIFE, I HAD TO ANSWER QUESTIONS—FROM INTERVIEWERS AND FROM MY ROOMMATES—ABOUT WHY I DID THINGS. I WAS ACTUALLY FORCED TO LOOK BACK AT MY BEHAVIOR AND RECALL MY ACTIONS AND DISSECT MY MOTIVATIONS.

definitely can be wild, and at school, there's a lot of binge drinking. I know that my tolerance got pretty high. I would drink from Thursday through Monday and not think about it.

But things were different when I got to Hawaii and into the house. I got caught off guard. I was acting like I always did, but something went wrong: I got alcohol poisoning. Lots of crazy things happen to me, and I get over them. But this time was different. Knowing that everyone was forming opinions of me—that this could be on TV—it changed everything. During the second week in Hawaii, Teck, Kaia, Matt, Justin, and I had an off-camera talk. We were in the kitchen having this secret conversation. The topic came up: How do you want to be

Well, I'm not just that. Teck's response was, "Actually, I'd peg you as 'the girl with a drinking problem.'" And then it hit me: *There's nowhere to go from here. Here are the labels. Here's how it's going to go.*

So on the second night of the show, my spirit broke. And for the next two months, it was like I was acting out of spite because I felt I had no choice. I was like, "F**k it, if this is what you think I am, I'll drink." And I did. I drank. A lot. Of course, underneath, I was hurting. I couldn't forgive myself for screwing up so early on. Everything started to go downhill. I was disappointed in myself, and I couldn't get past it. I wish I'd had a counselor then.

Before I knew it, I was kicked out of the house.

And for the month that I was gone, I wasn't sure what I was going to do. I'm so stubborn, I thought when I left the house I was leaving for good. I couldn't decide whether I should come back. But I realized there was all this stuff I shoulda woulda done. And I'm not a quitter. Unfortunately, there was so little time left. When it was time to move out, I felt like I was just getting started. I couldn't believe the time was over. The others, they felt like they'd just been through a marathon. But I was feeling fresh and ready for more.

The Real World caught me at a time when I was just learning about my past, just putting things together. There's a lot of anger I should feel toward things that happened in my childhood, but I don't want to. I want to turn any bitterness into positive motivation. Like, "Hey, Grandma, you think I can't do this. Watch me. You think I can't graduate college? Watch me." As I see it: the people in Manhattan high-rises, they believe in themselves. The people who work at McDonald's, they don't. It's all about changing your thinking. Which is why I'm so mad at myself for getting bogged down in the "You're going to be known as having a drinking problem" thing. I don't know why I couldn't learn from the second day, realize getting drunk was not the way to go, and just chill.

I learned so much from *The Real World*. And I think it'll change me forever. From now on, I'll be looking at my life as it happens. I just hope it won't be as dramatic anytime soon. I don't think I could take it!

The Real Word on... RUTHIE

TECK: Ruthie's very powerful. I don't think she understands her power. She's twenty-two, but she reminds me of an eighteen-year-old high school senior. She needs to grow up. When I first saw Ruthie, I thought she was a cute little Hawaiian girl. Then she told me about her upbringing and being gay and I thought, *mental case.* I thought she was dingy. It was too early to tell her she wasn't gay and just confused because she didn't have love in her life.

KAIA: Ruthie's an incredible woman. I feel her anger toward me now, based on the fact that I was part of a team of people who in her eyes "kicked her out." I worked hard at my friendship with Ruthie, and I think we built a foundation for the future. She's a beautiful girl.

JUSTIN: I don't think I know Ruthie that well. She's a nice girl, though. I wish her well.

COLIN: I admire the way Ruthie approaches life. I'm all for her shooting for the best things in life, but I think she should have a back-up plan. I don't think she grew up at all in Hawaii. She's still not responsive to advice. On another note, Ruthie sleeps with her eyes open. That is f**king scary.

MATT: If there's anyone who can match Teck with charisma, it's Ruthie. She wants to be an MTV veejay, and I don't know why she couldn't be. I hope that with her success, she's able to maintain stability. She has a tendency to let total strangers into her life.

AMAYA: I apologize to Ruthie for any misconceptions I've had. She can always be true to herself. I hope she remains happy and healthy. I thank her for giving me strength. Of everybody in the house, I most admire her for staying as real as she did.

RUTHiE: The alliances in the house were always changing. At this point in time, I think I'll keep in touch with everybody. I'll probably talk to Matt and Colin more than anyone else, though. Then Amaya.

from the CONTROL ROOM

Matt Kunitz, Supervising Producer: Ruthie is an amazing person. She had a hard time this season, but she triumphed in a major way. I'm very impressed with her. That said, Ruthie and I have a strange relationship. I think she sees me as the bad guy, as authoritarian. She's not someone who likes being told what to do. How she was raised made her feel like she was totally in control, and she does not like others in control. There are some rules on *The Real World:* You can't spend the night out of the house. You can't de-mike yourself. And you can't not return pages. Well, during a three-day stretch with Malo, Ruthie did all of those things. She was not living up to her commitment. I told her this, told her that if she were in a job, she'd have been fired. She broke down. She cried all afternoon and evening. She can't easily accept guidance or criticism.

JON Murray, Creator: Having cast Ruthie, I think we did the best we could letting Ruthie be Ruthie while still making sure she didn't hurt herself or anyone else.

MARY-ELLiS BUNiM, Creator: She was a strong presence in Hawaii, and now is very reluctant to admit that it actually happened the way we see it on air. Denial could be her downfall and I hope that doesn't happen. She has an opportunity to be a role model and I hope she'll eventually realize how many lives she's going to affect and change for the better.

'm not a fan of attention. I'm pretty sure by the time this book comes out, I'll have lost my anonymity. That scares me. I'm the writer type, the guy who steps away. I clearly remember my last day at UCLA. I took a twelve-minute walk and didn't run into one person I knew. Is that ever going to happen again?

I grew up in Del Mar, a Southern California suburb that borders on Rancho Santa Fe, an incredibly wealthy area, the upper one percent of America. There were houses around my area that made the Hawaii house look poor in comparison.

I took the contract I made with the producers of *The Real World* very seriously. I honored the process; I adhered to the rules; I didn't run away. Verbally, and in writing, I agreed to many things, among them: don't do drugs, be truthful, don't take off your mike, return directors' pages. It bothered me when the roommates weren't as serious about the rules as I was. I had a hunch that in interviews Teck was holding out information about having sex in the house. He was obviously having sex on a daily basis, and I resented that he wasn't open about it. I thought that was the point of the

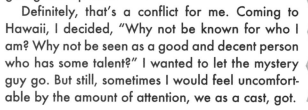

IN A RESTAURANT, EVERYONE WOULD BE POINTING AT US, COMING UP TO US, ASKING WHETHER WE WERE ON THE REAL WORLD. I'D BE LIKE, "IT'S NOT THE REAL WORLD. *WINK*. WE'RE DOING A DOCUMENTARY FOR THE WEATHER CHANNEL." OF COURSE, IF I WAS OUT WITH SOMEONE LIKE, SAY, TECK, HE'D BE LIKE "DAMN STRAIGHT, IT'S THE REAL WORLD."

I decided I wasn't going to get caught up in the "Let's just go nuts because our parents can afford it" lifestyle. In high school, I had a job at a radio station and a volunteer job with a children's theater group. I retreated from the scene. By senior year, people were saying to me, "Whoa, I didn't realize you still went to this school." People thought I was mysterious, and I enjoyed it. It was the same way at UCLA. I was the guy nobody really knew. I'm absolutely giving that up now.

Definitely, that's a conflict for me. Coming to Hawaii, I decided, "Why not be known for who I am? Why not be seen as a good and decent person who has some talent?" I wanted to let the mystery guy go. But still, sometimes I would feel uncomfortable by the amount of attention, we as a cast, got.

show. So when cameras were there, I'd confront him. I'd say point blank, "Define what 'chilling' is." Because he was always saying he was "chilling" with women, and I wanted that out there. I wanted him to say what that meant. Why was I so invested? Well, it's an uncomfortable predicament to feel like maybe you've gone too far, been too open, when there are others who haven't been documented fully.

Like Colin and Amaya. I don't have proof of it, but I think they made efforts to be private about their relationship. Well, that would be okay in a natural environment. But, this is not a natural environment. There may be certain things you don't want to reveal to the masses, but still....My feeling is, if you're going to have a private conversation, it should be documented.

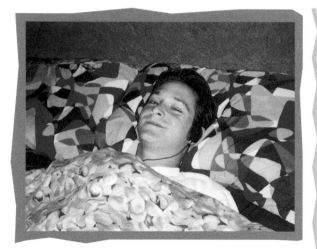

And if you're going to have an epiphany, it should be documented. That's what we're here for. As production was ending, I kept hearing roommates say, "Oh, remember that time we took off our mikes." That's so frustrating to me. I heard Kaia

would do that—take off her mike, vent about the roommates: then put it back on. God, I'm naive. Maybe I should have done that. Gone off, said a bunch of crap that nobody could hear, then come home all smiles. But no; in my mind, that unleveled the playing fields.

Maybe I'm approaching the show in a different way. Maybe it has to do with wanting to be a writer, and wanting to tell the best, realest story possible. Maybe it's because I have a TV mind.

Being interviewed weekly and knowing that your housemates are being interviewed weekly, that changes everything. I think emotions get magnified. You feel there's an immediacy to your situation. On interview days, it felt like life would stop. After you do interviews, you're all stirred up. It's all you can talk about. You're asked to confront feelings, pick apart situations. And that forces you into action. Of course you're going to end up fight-

The Real Word on...

AMAYA: When I first met Matt, I thought he had an edge. But then he became Mr. Rogers. Matt is a person I don't feel is entirely genuine. If he really was as nice as he appears to be, that would be amazing. He'd get a look on his face like there was a smart-ass comment lurking beneath the surface. Occasionally, it would come out. But usually he'd just mutter comments under his breath. He helped me in a couple of situations, like when I had a panic attack about my dad and the Colin situation.

RUTHIE: Matt's cool, but he's overbearing like a brother. He's a sweet guy, that's all. Of all the roommates, he's the only one who cared when I left the house.

TECK: Big brother Matt, he's always concerned. Sometimes that seemed fake, though he was pretty consistent. At first I was like, he can't be that right all the time.

KAIA: Matt attained a closeness with all of us because he's such a trusting individual. But I've heard him say he doesn't know what to believe, whom to take seriously. We've had amazing times together. He can be incredibly open and straightforward.

JUSTIN: Ninety-five percent of the time, Matt and I really jelled. Except for one drunken night, we always got along. In the house, everyone got along with him the most. There were times when I thought that there were fundamentally weak things about him. But now I think he's got his own way. He's a sweet guy.

COLIN: I enjoy Matt. I'm going to keep in touch with him. I'll probably see him a lot since we both live in Southern California. We have some similar interests. I'm not as interested in writing, but we both have goals that involve the entertainment industry.

ing. Amaya would always come back from interviews and be like, "I had a great interview. Why? I just talked s**t about everybody and it was so fun." I made it my policy to not say anything in my interviews that I wouldn't say to my roomates. The way I see it: You gotta take the high road. You gotta be mature. It's the same with talking behind people's backs. I never did that. I think that's weak. If that happened in our house, that's sad.

In life, you need to be honest with everyone. In the documentary environment, that's particularly true.

Matt: I'll talk to Colin the most. Then Teck. Then Ruthie. I have a desire to speak to Ruthie every day. Her life is extraordinarily compelling. Then Kaia. Then Justin. The only one I wonder about is Amaya. The ball's in her court.

from the CONTROL ROOM

Matt Kunitz, supervising producer: When we first started doing casting interviews, Matt told us he'd been a peer counselor in college. But Matt makes a point of getting involved in every situation. He fancies himself a producer, I think. He knows what makes good TV and what doesn't. That's great for him and his future. But not so great for us. For instance, he batphoned a director, Russ, to say he knew Russ wasn't getting something he wanted from Kaia in interviews. He said he'd get it. I told him, "Don't get anything for us. The best thing you could do for yourself is to live your life without thinking about us at all."

Mary-Ellis Bunim, creator: Matt is a chameleon, reflecting whatever needs to color the moment. He's always got to be in control, to be the final arbitrator.

Jon Murray, creator: I think Matt will be surprised by some of the aspects of his personality the cameras picked up.

KAIA

With *The Real World* over, I feel incredible. I am thoroughly satisfied, like I'm made for life. I consider my time in Hawaii as part of a lifelong process of self-examination. I've managed to become more self-aware since this started and I've tried to encourage other women to be that way.

From day one, I loved having the cameras around me. Production warned us that after a while we wouldn't like the attention, but that never happened. I loved the cameras. They helped me to recognize the strength and importance of my voice. I saw other people have moments when they were uncomfortable, like when they were meeting

I initially thought Amaya was shallow and petty, but I still wanted to find something more in her.

I saw during my time in Hawaii that people were scared of me. That's happened to me a lot in my life. I'm used to it. The funny thing is I think being strong is both my weakness and my strength. People think I don't need help or love or support. I do. But it's hard for me to tell people what I want from them.

If this process taught me anything, it's this: live your life in an honest way. You have no choice but to show who you are. I wish Justin had realized that. I know it was hard for him, but he didn't embrace the show and, as a result, the show didn't

I WAS THE MOST HONEST PERSON IN THE HOUSE. AND I WAS THE PERSON WHO MOST TRIED TO GET TO KNOW OTHER PEOPLE. ALL I WANT TO DO IN LIFE IS BE CREATIVE AND EXPLORE PEOPLE'S PERSONALITIES. BEING IN HAWAII ALLOWED ME TO DO BOTH OF THOSE THINGS.

people for the first time. But I didn't have moments like that. I never stopped loving the cameras.

I learned a lot about the people living with me. Ruthie said to me once, "I wish you were the Kaia I thought you were when I first got to Hawaii." Well, who did she think I was? She never got a chance to see the whole me. You know, it really wasn't until the end of the show that I was able to begin expressing my silly side—and I do have one. We had a lot of serious things to deal

with in the few months we were there, and it just didn't get a chance to come out. My roommates are guilty of not getting to know each other in the most real ways. I really tried, though. I did. For example,

embrace him. It makes sense that the roommates occasionally get angry at the production staff and get scared, but if you don't like the way you're portrayed on the show it's because you don't like who you are in this environment. I'm not scared of anything that might end up on the show. I have nothing to be ashamed of and nothing to hide.

I'd never watched *The Real World*, so all I knew going into the house was that I was me. Well, the house definitely provided me with new ways of looking at things, new perspectives. I am an only child and I'd never shared a room before. I'd also never held myself accountable to anybody else before. I never had to tell my mom

where I was going. In Hawaii, you had to tell people where you were. You had to keep the directors and producers informed. You had to tell your roommates when you had the car. I liked that. I liked people caring where I was.

I know that I come off as opinionated and real-ly confident, and maybe that has to do with how I was raised. My parents were both self-imagined people. They were separated when I was two and officially divorced when I was eight. They talked all the time after that. A lot about me. They really cared about my development as a person. My dad died when I was eighteen, but I think he would be really proud to know that I was on *The Real World*. He always encouraged me to travel and meet people. And he'd be most proud if he thought that on *The Real World* I was spreading positive messages.

The Real Word on... Kaia

MATT: Kaia is as strong a woman as I've ever met. At times her strength can be misinterpreted as selfishness. At first I didn't realize she was sweet, but she is. If you take the time to get to know her, she will show more of a goofy side. She's a fantastic artist and amazing poet, who unfortunately can close herself off emotionally.

RUTHIE: Kaia's such an actress. She told me all she wanted to do is spend the summer with me. She's just like that. She'll tell you something she doesn't mean. It cracks me up when she tells me deep things. What she says and the way she acts are two totally different things. At the beginning we were friends. I wish she was the Kaia I thought she was. She's always contradicting herself. She'll stick up for me, but then she'll do something like go back in a club after I'm kicked out. I feel like in some ways she's selfish. She walks around with her nose in the air and can't get over herself.

TECK: Kaia, well, what can I say: once a bitch, always a bitch. But she's a good bitch. Kaia, that's my girl. She's my best friend in the house. We'll definitely stay friends. Kaia's ghetto. She has no class. She's the type of person who'll take your stuff, and then matter-of-factly be like, "Oh, I took it." That's the type of person she is. Ghetto. But she's a sweetheart.

JUSTIN: I wish Kaia well. I worry about her. She's extremely talented. She has an energy and an awareness and a singular way of looking at things. The way she tells a story is fantastic and that's such a talent. Knowing that she doesn't know what she's going to do after the show worries me. I'm scared of her getting overwhelmed by her talent and where to go with it. I would definitely have sought to be Kaia's friend if we weren't living in the house. She's a phenomenal person. It's too bad things went so awry for us.

AMAYA: Off camera, Kaia's nice, especially if she's trying to get something from you. On camera, she's very serious and deep. She's always trying to feel you and it's always very intense. The conversation could be about you, but it would always turn back to her. I learned to trust Kaia and we were friends for a little bit. But will I be friends with her again? Oh God, no. Of anybody, she turned on me the most.

COLIN: At the end of the show, I saw Kaia laugh and smile a lot. When she's lighthearted, she's so cute. But most of the time she's intense and deep. Toward the end of the process, she was not so analytical. I'm definitely on good terms with her. But I do have a negative thing to say: Kaia does not wear deodorant. She can really reek sometimes. She knows it, too.

If viewers watch this, and think it's not real, well, they're wrong. Our interactions are totally real. Sure, people are conscious of the cameras. How can they not be? And, yes, people want to look a certain way at certain times. But what's wrong with portraying yourself as you want to be, and then becoming that person? Of course, I won't be able to choose how people perceive me. But I hope viewers see me as an honest, strong, charismatic, and loving friend. Oh, and put "passionate" in there, too.

STAYING IN TOUCH

Kaia: At the end I was closest to Teck. Then Matt. Then Colin. I'll keep in touch with all of them. Ruthie, I hope I'll talk to. Justin, I'm not sure, and Amaya, probably not.

from the CONTROL ROOM

Matt Kunitz, Supervising Producer: Kaia enjoyed this process more than anything. She loves herself. She's an exhibitionist. And *The Real World* is an exhibitionist's dream.

Mary-Ellis Bunim, Creator: Kaia continuously surprised me by being exactly who she says she is. There's certainly no shortage of confidence or ego, but Kaia has the goods to back up the bravado.

Jon Murray, Creator: What makes Kaia so interesting as a cast member is that as much as she talks about herself, she never fully reveals her whole self. I think that's because she's still figuring out who she is. As for the lighter, funnier side of Kaia, viewers will have a chance to see it in the home video *The Real World You Never Saw: Hawaii.*

JUSTIN

he irony of *The Real World* is that the producers hope to see the cast members experience growth and evolution, yet the whole process is tainted with a heavy sense of fatalism. By that I mean that it's really difficult to grow when you feel like you're filling a slot. I had a nagging suspicion that coming on the show, I was filling a quota. I feel as though I was supposed to play a certain character, and short of something miraculous, it was impossible to get beyond that. It was hard to evolve in the house. Within three weeks, whatever you'd been able to give was it. I felt pegged by my roommates. It was hard to demonstrate being well-rounded. In part, I

age doesn't think about celebrity and media? Why are there so many applicants to the show? Because people want to be famous, they want to be part of the machine. Well, word to the wise: if there's any cure-all for that, it's being on *The Real World*. The experience of being taped all the time—you really have no idea how dehumanizing it's going to be until you live it.

In the beginning, I was actually happy to be in Hawaii. I was having a little internal renaissance. I did get to do my writing and reading—proof being the hours of footage they have of me with a book in my hand. As for my roommates, I experienced the house as a game of sorts. I considered *The*

> I DIDN'T DO WHAT TECK DID. HE FELT HE HAD TO LEAVE THE HOUSE TO HAVE TIME TO HIMSELF. I WASN'T WILLING TO DO THAT. I SPENT TIME IN THE HOUSE, BUT IT WAS QUIET TIME. BUT I GUESS PEOPLE INTERPRETED MY SILENCE AS SOMETHING MORE THAN JUST THAT.

blame the cameras for that. They create a tension that forces people to either be disingenuous or silent.

What did I think *The Real World* was going to be? Frankly, I had no idea what to expect. I'd only seen a few episodes—like maybe one from five of the previous seasons. It seemed to me like an appealing and unique experience, one that I urgently needed. I'd been top heavy on the intellectual agenda, and I felt I needed to take a break from my life for a little introspection, to retreat to more holistic pursuits. That's why I went to Hawaii: to do some regrouping, to write and read, to have a vacation.

Okay, I admit there's another constellation of features that made me do *The Real World*. I study media and sociology, so that added an interesting element to the process. And, yes, there was some sort of hubris about getting on. I mean, who in this

Real World a vacation from my life, and I didn't really have a desire to know any of my roommates too well. Kaia was a surprise. I didn't think there'd be someone I wanted to really know, so that was a pleasant little shock. And Matt was a good guy. But, other than that, I was happy to keep my distance. It wasn't that I was being snotty or dismissive, it was just that I wasn't outgoing. And, by the way, that's how I am in my real life. I wouldn't say that the roommates saw the best part of me. I hold some of my actions accountable for that. But I'm also the type of person in whom it takes a long time to see the good. I usually don't try to call attention to it.

I never thought about the show airing, so I didn't think about how things would appear. Honestly, I didn't care about my representation. None of my friends watch the show. And it's also

significant that I was the only person in the house who didn't have aspirations to a media career. Frankly, by week two, I thought I'd faded away into the background. And actually I feel, I was basically silent for the first two months. But I'm sure I got sucked into story lines. Especially with Amaya and Colin in a bed above me. I couldn't help being a part of that. I wouldn't be honest if I didn't admit that I'm nervous about the show and how it's going to come out. It's true that they can't tell the *whole* story, but I didn't go on the show to have a story told about me. I feel there's going to be a lot of speculation about my departure. And I think the roommates are going to talk a lot about Kaia's and my tendencies toward manipulation. Was I ever manipulative in the house? Yes. But there's nothing patently original about my behavior. I mean, who wouldn't label Amaya's behavior at times manipulative? In a very small fashion I think we've all got those tendencies. If I feel anything it's that I came off badly because I was more honest than the rest.

In the end, I did get good things out of being in Hawaii. I was able to remember that the world is wide open if you're a person who's willing to try and grab for it. And I was able to kind of stand above the rat maze and see the whole outline. I looked a lot at myself: the good parts, the bad parts. It was a reunion of sorts—with myself.

The Real Word on... **JUSTiN**

TECK: Justin has a quiet, dark side. I saw the dark side and the light side. With me, he was never dishonest or shady. He probably talked about a brother behind his back, but face-to-face, it was all good.

AMAYA: I think that I could never consider Justin a good friend. He needs to step back and have some fun. The fact that he was denied a lot of childhood experiences has affected him negatively. I do admire that he fights hard for causes, but I don't identify with him at all. Wanna hear a funny thing about him? He gets a weird smile on his face before he gets mad. Like he's about to laugh. It's very menacing. Come to think of it, he could be from a different planet. I'd definitely buy that.

MATT: I see Justin as a very smart guy. I think at times he was very misunderstood. We had many deep and intellectual conversations. I see him as a good guy who was at a loss in the house.

RUTHIE: The only thing I have to say about Justin is that I still don't know who he is. He's the great manipulator to me. He's so smart, he's dangerous. He could just not be gay for all I know.

KAIA: I'm confused about Justin. Justin and I knew each other really well. In fact, I'd say I knew him best. We mutually needed each other. We needed to talk about politics or societal issues. There was constant intellectual jousting. I've shown him a lot of trust and respect, I think. Our friendship was beautiful, and there was a lot of life and growth that came out of it. But still, I needed to separate from him.

COLIN: Sometimes I felt like Justin was speaking in another language. Maybe he was talking pig Latin. I have a real problem with basing intelligence solely on book smarts. It's ridiculous and upsetting that how smart you are is defined by what words you use. He's poor at social interaction. Doesn't that count for anything?

JUSTIN: For now I'm content with keeping my distance from everyone in the house. Perhaps I'll e-mail with Matt.

from the CONTROL ROOM

Matt Kunitz, Supervising Producer: Viewers will see very little of Justin on the show. Why? No. 1: He didn't make himself available to the roommates. And No. 2: He looked too deeply into the process, studying its machinations. Instead of involving himself with the roommates, with his life in Hawaii, he was wondering: "What are this director's intentions? Why is there a camera there?" If you're self-editing, this project is impossible. If you can throw up your hands—just be yourself—doing *The Real World* becomes infinitely easier. Justin was paranoid that he was being typecast to fill a role. All we ever ask is that you be yourself.

Mary-Ellis Bunim, Creator: Justin created his own reality and his own self-fulfilling prophecy, by approaching the show as if creating a role. No one can sustain a role for five months and Justin, eventually exposed by his roommates, could only do one thing—leave the show.

Jon Murray, Creator: Justin never really gave most of his roommates or the show a chance. He could have learned a lot. He could have also had a lot of fun. Too bad!

THE BEGINNING

First Impressions

AMAYA: I'M NOT USED TO MEETING PEOPLE IN THE BUFF FOR THE FIRST TIME, SO IT WAS A LITTLE WEIRD TO WALK IN THE HOUSE AND IMMEDIATELY GET ACQUAINTED WITH TECK'S PENIS—NOT TO MENTION RUTHIE'S BOOBS AND CHA CHA.

I was kinda just hoping that I'd be walking up to the house and shaking hands with people, not trying to avoid looking at body parts. Of course, Teck came up and gave me a big wet naked hug, and I had to think about his thing on my leg. So, my first impressions are pretty jumbled. I immediately thought Justin was cute and quiet, so quiet I almost thought that he didn't like us at

first. Kaia is an intimidating person when you first meet her. She's very strong and very confident, but she seems to have this really kind of cute side to her. Matt's not my type but he's definitely a cute guy. He's certainly very nice and very approachable. I've never encountered such an accommodating human being. I keep telling him if he acts that way so much, he's going to get walked all over. Colin, I was shocked to see him. I did not like him in any way shape or form when I met him on the casting follow. I thought he was obnoxious and very surface-y. I just could not stand him. But Colin is actually a very nice guy and because I am getting to know him more and more, I'm liking him more and more.

JUSTIN: My initial first impressions? Amaya, for all her issues, has a fun vibe and makes me laugh. Ruthie is kind of problematic, but sweet. Colin is young and well-intentioned, and I hope in the future he comes to realize and understand the entitlement he walks around with. Matt is looking very hard for something and along the way he's just the nicest guy. Teck, I hope his illusions don't all collapse so that he cracks. And Kaia's just the bomb. Kaia has a very indomitable sense of self, which is why I think we get along so well.

RUTHIE: Justin is the gay version of James Dean, with more style. Amaya is the sorority girl, blonde chick, blue-eyed, "I-want-your-attention-at-all-times" type of girl. She's gonna kill me. Matt is: "When I get to know you, I'll be there for you like a brother and you can count on me always." Colin is "I need to look good and take care of my body and I'm a mama's boy." Kaia is a mysterious vegan who's real sweet at times, but you never really know what she's thinking. And Teck is the self-proclaimed daddy of the house.

Kaia: Teck is the type of person who will be able to hang with me at any point. His eyes are open really wide and he's taking in every second and I appreciate that greatly. My first impression of Amaya is sorority chick, Valley girl, uptight. My initial reaction: "This chick isn't about to take her clothes off." I also know when I see Amaya, immediately, that she's not secure about her body because of her slouch. There are walls up around her that are very different from my walls. Justin seems to be a brilliant, interesting, amorphous character. My first impression of Matt is that he's a very chill, relaxed, watching-things-and-taking-things-in type of dude. We vibe instantly in a way that is not normal for me. My first impression of Ruthie is, a chick with flavor. I'm seeing a naked woman and I'm thinking, this is a beautiful naked woman. I'm really happy because I really wanted there to be another beautiful woman.

Matt: Amaya and I right off the get-go had no trouble conversing. She's blessed with the gift of gab. I did a lot of listening and got to know a lot about her sorority. I found her to be very beautiful and very interesting. My first impression of Colin is that he is a guy who's into himself, into the way he looks, probably works out a lot, but I don't know if he's ever been tested emotionally. I look into his eyes and don't see a great deal of experience. My first impression is that Kaia cares about Kaia. As long as Kaia's happy, Kaia's cool. Kaia is real. She is someone I will be able to trust 'cause she's never gonna mask what's on her mind. I look at her and right away I think there is nothing that is going to

happen between me and Kaia sexually. Nothing. There will not be a time when I'm attracted to her. And, because of that, I started to feel comfortable right away. Justin struck me as someone on my level. Justin looks like a guy who's got a lot more on his mind than sports and sex, whereas I can tell that Teck is sex, sex, sex all the time and maybe Colin is sports, sports, sports all the time. Justin, I feel, hey, I gotta chance to talk about poetry with this guy. I'm talking to Ruthie and I'm thinking she is so pretty, she is so interesting and alluring, I would like to get to know her on a semi or more intimate level. And then she tells me "I'm bisexual and attached to a female at the moment." And my interest level fades fast.

Teck: I met Ruthie first. What did I think? In one sentence Ruthie is: I love life, but I'm so confused I'll do anything as long as someone talks me into it, period. My first impression of Amaya? Well, I just can't get past her chest. I mean, it just hits me. It hits me like so hard, like bam in the head, like damn, she has some nice breasts. But I managed to talk to her. Amaya is your typical UCLA sorority girl, period. And Matt, he's the good American wholesome white boy, which is cool 'cause you need one of those around in every household. Kaia is real brash when I meet her. She's someone who has her guard up, but she's cool. Justin is an observer. He kind of sits back and just looks at everything. Just as long as he don't get on the rooftop and start snipin' people, we'll be all right. And, Colin, he's a cool cat. We had a nice time when we met in casting. We were the funky pimps. If you talk to women and you're down with me on that level, you're all right with me.

COLIN: I hadn't met Matt, Justin, or Ruthie before I got on the show. The first thing I remember Ruthie saying is that she's a chain-smoker and has a drinking problem. So, right off the bat she was open with me. Matt, I connected with him right off the bat. He reminds me a lot of my best friend, Trevor.

He's very modest. Teck and I had had a great time, so we were happy to see each other. And Kaia, I was shocked to see that she was picked for the show because, in my mind, I didn't think they would pick two people from the same school. And we both go to Berkeley. I thought Amaya was weird in her interview, so I was indifferent to her being there. And Justin stood back, acted a little sinister.

THE
LOVE

Ruthie & Jess

Ruthie: I met Jess in January 1998. She was going out with a friend of mine, a guy actually, who's going to kill me when he sees the show. He's gonna watch the show and be like, "F**kin' Bitch!" He has no idea we got together. We're both bisexual, but I don't think he knew that!

The thing I most loved about Jess was her heart. She's got a really really big heart. She's very sensitive and romantic and I loved that. She's always full of surprises and she treated me well. We were together a year and a few months before we broke up. Why we broke up has nothing to do with the show. Or, by the way, with Malo. It's just that Jess asked me to marry her. I couldn't say yes. I mean, I just wasn't sure. If you're not sure, that means no.

Why wasn't I sure? Well, Jess still thinks about other people. Plus, she's only eighteen. I decided to let the relationship go but not the friendship. Jess and I are very, very opposite. I love her, but I wasn't sure anymore if I was in love with her and that's why I broke it off. I can't live in a relationship that's a lie, and partially it was. I still think she's sweet and amazing on the phone, I have to try not to melt when I talk to her.

Kaia and Matt came and talked to me about why I broke up with Jess. They were asking me why. I was like, "Why do you have to know?" Matt said he felt like he needed validation; he felt like he'd heard all about the relationship and wanted to understand. I didn't understand why it was any of his business. Roommates...!

Ruthie & Kaia

RUTHIE: Early on in the house, Kaia told me that she was attracted to dark-skinned Hawaiian guys. We were at Don Ho's, I think. Anyway, I joked back, "Yeah, well, what about me?" She was like, "You know I'm attracted to you." Right then and there, I made like I didn't hear her.

But, of course, we ended up kissing—although I don't remember. I remember this one kiss at this club Liquids, and it was just, you know, a jokey joke. Like what I'd do with my friends in Jersey. The kiss in the van that everyone was talking about, I still don't remember it. But, I'm sure I

did it for a reason. It's funny now, but at the time it was really scary that I didn't remember it. Word is I also made out with a guy that night. Anyway, the kiss with Kaia is when it started to get serious about the blackouts. I remember everything before and everything after the pictures they have. I like the fact that I'm covering my face in the pictures. At least I'm a smarty when I'm blacking out.

Kaia and I stopped talking to each other for a little bit after the kiss. We were avoiding each other because everyone kept asking us whether there was a relationship.

Kaia: It's not like in the van was the only time we kissed. The reason it seemed like such a big deal was that the cameras were there. I didn't think it

was that monumental. During the kiss, she held my head toward her and said, "This is the real world." Others have confirmed that story for me. I'm not saying she didn't want to kiss me, but she was definitely interested in cameras.

I was drunk that night too, but I remember how it started. Earlier in the night, someone gave me a piece of paper with a phone number on it for Ruthie. I gave it to her, and then some random person, a friend of Ruthie's from high school or something, screamed, "Throw it away, 'cause Ruthie needs to think about Jess!" The next thing I know I'm in the car saying, "F**k Jess." And then Ruthie was kissing me. It was fine with me. I had no problem with it. I was attracted to her and it felt good. But it quickly became not good because I felt like Ruthie was doing it more for the spectacle and less for her own enjoyment.

Matt Kunitz, Supervising Producer: When viewers rewatch the episode they'll notice that when Kaia and Ruthie began kissing, our camera was not in the van. Fortunately, they got stuck at a red light, allowing our cameraman, Jorge, to jump into the van. Kaia and Ruthie were so into each other, they hardly noticed Jorge's sudden appearance.

Teck & the Ladies

TECK: AT THIS POINT IN MY LIFE, I LIKE HOOCHIES. TIGHT-CLOTHED, COCKTAIL-DRINKING, CHEAP-SHOE-WEARING, FAKE-LOUIS-VUITTON-SPORTING WOMEN.

My ideal type of woman has to have a phat fat ass, a good family background, a bomb-ass CD collection, and goals. She needs to be a big thinker like me. She also has to know how to cook.

I never wanted to get together with someone in the house. Of course, I wanted to flirt, but I'll never get with them. Kaia was hesitant enough about leaving my room when I had company. Imagine if we'd gotten together. I would never have gotten her out of there!

RUTHIE: Teck, I don't know what girls see in him. At least he gets what he wants. Sometimes you'd pass his bed and just see a t*t hanging out.

Kaia: I love Teck, but there's one contradiction in my mind. I believe in quality and not quantity in relationships. With Teck, there was not a lot of quality being exchanged between him and his pals.

The Definitions

HANGING OUT:
Getting to know someone, no sex.

CHILLING:
Spending time with a person, but there's the likelihood of sex in the air. You can smell it like a Chili's fajita.

SEEING SOMEONE:
When you get your freak on daily.

Teck's True Confession

TECK: I did have a crush on a crew member. Man, I was in love with one of the directors, Teri. I was so attracted to Teri that I could barely look at her. I knew that I couldn't talk to her for more than two minutes. Otherwise, I would have to make a move. When I had to call on the batphone, I'd love it when she answered the phone, but I'd hate it at the same time. She just made me so nervous. I most hated when Teri would follow me when I was with a girl. Most of the time I wasn't thinking about who I was with, but when Teri was with me I was hyper-conscious of my company. Mainly because I wanted to be with her. She would put that camera on her shoulder and it was so sexy. She'd have these raggedy Levi's on and her shirt would ride up. She was so hot, it was to the point that I couldn't even look at her. I think she liked me, too. I saw it in her eyes.

COLIN: Teck has a crush on a crew member? Just one crew member? He got drunk on his birthday, like really really drunk. He started screaming about how he wanted to suck one of the crew members' toes. And that's not even the one he said he had a crush on!

Amaya & Colin

AMAYA: It was on the second night that I started sleeping in Colin's bed. That was the night Ruthie went to the hospital. I was feeling really scared and wanted someone to hold me. We'd been talking about how we liked sleeping next to another person, and that's kind of how it happened. I know it sounds fishy, but that first night was really innocent. It was just sleeping.

I guess it was the next night that we started kissing. We were both pretty nervous. I was thinking, "Is this a good idea?" He's a sweet kisser, though. From that first kiss, we decided to be secret about it—both from production and the roommates. Obviously, everyone knew we were sleeping together, but we were incognito about it. Justin was the first to know we were fooling around, because, duh, he was right there in the bottom bunk. He was always getting mad. Then Matt started asking questions. He's that kind of guy. He watches stuff. Anyway, we managed to keep things secret for a while. But, then, I don't know, we brought it into the open. Like on Valentine's Day, when Colin made that really bold move of putting gifts on my bed. Colin thought it was unfair to the process and to production to hide our relationship. He said we'd made an agreement. That's one of the reasons we opened up.

We had so much fun in bed. The best thing about sleeping in bed with him was laughing at night. We'd laugh so hard, we'd have to put our heads in the pillow, so we didn't wake everyone else up. And on a serious note, we learned a lot

JUSTIN: ALL I HAVE TO SAY ABOUT COLIN AND AMAYA IS: WOULD YOU WANT TO SLEEP UNDER THAT? I THINK ALL OF AMERICA WOULD GIVE THE SAME ANSWER—NO.

about each other. We'd vent to each other about things going on in the house.

Our best times were always when we were by ourselves. The fact is, the other roommates brought in a real negative factor. In front of them, we'd be trying to pretend like something wasn't happening. We'd end up being rude to each other just so they wouldn't catch on. And once it was out in the open, it suddenly became everyone's relationship. It wasn't the cameras that were a problem as much as the roommates.

If there hadn't been so much scrutiny, if we'd just been regular people, the relationship would probably have worked out differently. But, as it was, it lasted a couple of months

COLIN: I DON'T LIKE TO BE WITH MY GIRLFRIEND IN FRONT OF MY FRIENDS, BECAUSE I ACT DIFFERENTLY WITH MY GIRLFRIEND. SO IT WAS VERY PECULIAR. I WAS VERY UNCOMFORTABLE.

and then ended. It was over the week my father got sick. That week, I felt vulnerable. I clung to Colin. And you know what? He was wonderful. He'd talk to me all the time. But I was just very needy and emotional. I have a feeling he was freaked out by how he was feeling.

It took a long time to really end the relationship. But then I started dating other people. For the record I just want to say that the Tony thing was much more innocent then anyone thinks. After Colin went to sleep, we talked for six or seven hours. Yes, we kissed, but more than that we talked. Still, it was a bad idea. I wasn't thinking. Kaia and Matt told Colin they thought I'd slept with Tony. That's not true. Still, I apologize for hurting Colin.

He made me feel very beautiful. This sounds crazy, but he'd say, "I love your butt." No one says that to me, because I have a weird butt. He'd

tell me I was what a woman should look like. He wasn't one for endearments. He'd make fun of my laugh, which is fair enough since I have an annoying high-pitched honking-type laugh.

I guess what I'll miss most is Colin's weird sense of humor. Oh, and I'll miss punching him. He's a really good person, but there were so many things against us. I don't think I'll ever be with Colin again. Romantically speaking, it's over. And now we're in the process of mending.

TECK: Colin and Amaya, that was great. They were a great water-cooler topic at the house. I don't know if they ever really broke up, since they were sharing a room for the last few weeks. Think about it: those lonely nights and lonely mornings and all those lonely moments in between. If Colin is anything like me, once you hit it, you can always hit it again.

Kaia: Amaya and Colin were very far removed from me. I didn't interact with them. It turned me off initially that they paired up immediately. I was more interested on focusing on people who were more willing to connect.

Ruthie: Amaya picked Colin the instant she saw him. You could see it in her eyes: "He's mine." And she's a chaser. I think she's the type of girl who, when she picks a guy, she usually gets him. I think under different circumstances Colin and Amaya could have worked out. But he's young. I don't think anyone should be mad, though I do know he was hurt by her. He just won't admit it. He told us once, "We've all been used and hurt by Amaya." I was like, "We have?" It made me wonder. I was thinking, "Gee, Colin, maybe it was you who was the most hurt." Colin wants justification. The situation made him look like an assh**e, and he isn't one.

Matt: There was a time when Colin came to me and explained all his frustrations with Amaya. I understood then and there that he was done with the relationship. The next morning, he broke up with her. Then she comes to me in a dreadful state, saying her dad is ill, and she can't eat. I tried to support her. I tried to be kind. I said, "Look, maybe you guys will get back together." In retrospect, I think that might have been perceived as Colin telling me one thing and me telling Amaya something else. I was doing my best to lend an ear and be supportive, but it wasn't always smoothly done.

COLIN: If you think it's hard to have an intimate conversation on camera, try having one with a woman you're involved with. And kissing on camera? That wasn't easy either. It's pretty eighth-grade to kiss people in public. That's not my thing. But in front of

a camera? That's a whole other story. Not only is there a camera, there's a person holding the camera, a person I sort of know. Since when did making out become a spectacle?

Remember one key phrase when talking about how my relationship with Amaya began: *She* slept in *my* bed. She went after me. At the beginning, I was straight-up with her. I didn't want a serious relationship. But we started something anyway. It was really against my better judgment. Although the cameras add a crazy element to the relationship, they were not my issue. It was just an "Oh my God, what have I gotten myself into?" type of thing. All of a sudden, I was in a relationship, a live-in one. People don't move in together after one date, but Amaya and I, that was our situation, we were already living together in this house. And that seriously hindered our relationship.

Aside from that, when we were in front of the roommates, our interaction sucked.

Amaya's more dependent than I am. She needed me to talk her through stuff—serious stuff. For instance, there were definitely times when she didn't want to stay in the house. I didn't want her to leave, but at the same time I felt responsible for her happiness in the house. I didn't like that. I felt guilty all the time. She would get pretty dramatic, pretty freaky over petty stuff, and I realized if she kept acting like this, my time in Hawaii would be ruined. That's when I knew the only thing we could be was friends.

Of course, she wasn't okay with that. Personally, I don't understand how that can happen. If one person says we can't be anything more than friends, then that's how it goes. She just wouldn't have it. I got mad. I told her, "At this point in our lives, it's not easy to be friends with you. Your negativity and fluctuating moods are too much."

Of course, when we separated, I missed Amaya and the romantic times we spent together. I missed sleeping with her at night, holding her, having her be happy. Matt suggested that our relationship was purely a physical thing. It had nothing to do with anything that's physical. Well, not nothing, but the fact was, I cared for her. I liked spending time with her. I liked going out with Amaya. I loved being around her. She was a great person when we were alone.

So, the whole thing was hard. But I had to remove myself from the situation. Amaya and I, we're just not right for each other. She's a beautiful person, though.

from the CONTROL ROOM

Matt Kunitz, Supervising Producer: Colin and Amaya, I never would have guessed it would happen, but I was thrilled. *Road Rules* always has relationships. We never do. *Road Rules* is more like summer camp—every day there's a group bonding experience; whereas on *The Real World,* it's more "live your lives and see what happens." It's easier to splinter off.

I'd say we as a production were there from the beginning of the relationship to the end—and unfortunately it was a nasty end. Colin and Amaya were incredibly cooperative with production. Then again, they had this bad habit of calling to get demiked, then getting into bed and talking for hours. We were missing all of that. Of course, I didn't want to hide a mike in their bed. That's beyond the call. So, what we did was put it out in the open, right above the bed. We wanted them to see it. Of course, Amaya batphoned immediately to tell us how sick we were. I said, "Listen, we don't want to hear you having sex, but we don't want to miss all these important conversations, either." It was a difficult quandary.

Mary-Ellis Bunim, Creator: All season I looked forward to the daily highlights reel that I would be sent from Hawaii to keep us up-to-date. These were an hour or so of great moments from the day before. Colin and Amaya dominated those reels—their relationship was a total roller coaster of emotion, charming and funny and sometimes disturbing. I wish I could release the uncut version!

Jon Murray, Creator: I will be eternally grateful to Colin and Amaya for giving us our first on-camera romance between two *Real World* cast members. Why it took eight seasons to get such a romance, I'll never know.

The Teck-Malo-Ruthie Triangle

MALO: I've decided to come clean. When *The Real World* was in Hawaii, I got involved with two cast members, Teck and Ruthie. And it made my life horrible.

I met Ruthie during the time she was kicked off the show. Actually, we went to the *Baywatch* auditions together. After that, a mutual friend confided in me, "I think Ruthie likes you." You know how you feel when you really like someone and you hear they like you? You get that tingly feeling. That's

thing, we just knew where we stood. But when she got back to the house, it turned bad. I didn't necessarily think that what we had—whatever it was—was something that neeeded to be flaunted. I wasn't embarrassed, but I was seriously confused. Ruthie said she didn't want a relationship, but she acted like we were in one.

I told Ruthie to keep it on the down low, but she didn't do it. She talked about us in interviews. I was really upset. And then her roommates, Matt and

TECK: IF YOU WRITE ABOUT MALO, KEEP HER IN RUTHIE'S SECTION. I DIDN'T BRING HER HOME. I KEPT HER IN THE DARK.

what happened to me. The thing is, I'd never been attracted to girls. I'd never even considered them. I mean, I've been around lots of beautiful women, but there was nothing. So to me, this was pretty crazy. Actually, with Ruthie, it was more than attraction. I just felt an intense connection.

Ruthie knew I had been hanging out with Teck. Yeah, Teck and I went out on some dates. And I'm not going to lie, I liked Teck. But I knew the type of guy he was. He straight out told me I wouldn't be the only one. We were just fooling around, me and Teck, but I kind of developed more feelings for him. Actually, I fell for him. But I knew it was one-sided, me for him.

Teck was away in India when I got to know Ruthie. I remember Ruthie's and my first kiss. We went to see the movie *Life*. I was flirting with her. I laid my head against her shoulder. She told me that she wanted to kiss me, but she didn't know how I'd react, since she knew I was straight. She looked into my eyes, and I looked into hers. And then I had my first kiss with a girl. From then on, I was attached.

We were never in a relationship, but we were really happy. It was like we didn't have to say any-

Kaia, told her that I was still seeing Teck. I admit we were still keeping in touch. But we were still friends. It was very confusing. I don't think that anybody in that house liked me. Matt and Kaia pretended to be my friends at first, but they turned on me really fast.

When Teck first saw me in the house with Ruthie, he was hurtful. "Oh, so you finally got into the house," he teased. He acted like I was just following the cameras. Well, I didn't want to be in front of cameras. I wanted to be on the down low. Teck and I had been on the down low in front of the cameras. I'd never even seen them. Yes, once, I had asked him to introduce me to his roommates. But when he said no, that he wanted to keep me to himself, I didn't care. I never asked to go and see the house. It wasn't a big deal for me.

I think Ruthie was jealous of Teck. She'd tease me and say, "I know you're here just to see Teck." But if I'd wanted to see Teck, I could have seen Teck. Everything got out of hand. And if I called for Ruthie, and Teck answered and we started talking, she'd get upset. Even her roommates got upset. Matt told me I had to come down to Local Motion to choose between Teck and Ruthie. But I'd already made my choice—Ruthie. I just still wanted to hide it.

Well, you know what? I'm not very good at hiding stuff. I totally played myself on that show. Of course, they caught us kissing. Of course, everyone knew. And I got really paranoid. I had horrible insomnia. Then, Ruthie stopped talking to me. The thing that hurt me most was that she believed Matt and Kaia over me. They told her I was still seeing Teck, and she believed them. That hurt me really bad. I went to the house to pick up my stuff. That was that. I felt completely betrayed by Ruthie. I didn't trust her. I was very afraid of her. I knew she could tell everything to everybody about me. But I still had powerful emotions for her.

But then, just before she was about to leave, we had this big talk, and she apologized for everything. That's why I went to the airport to say good-bye to her. All of a sudden, I knew that

World is part of Ruthie's life, she can't help it.

Teck's good on the sexual level, but he's not good about making you feel good inside. He didn't show me anything new. With Ruthie, everything was new. She appreciated me. She wanted me for me and not the way I looked. There have been a lot of guys who have tried to play me, you know. I've met a lot of Tecks in my life. I've met only one Ruthie.

Matt: Malo, man, she's a piece of work. To me, Malo was a camera slut. I'm not questioning that she fell in love with Ruthie. I believe that. Hey, I slept in the bed next to them....

There's no denying that Malo was drawn to the cameras—despite the fact the second she got into our house she got reamed. Everyone in the house thought she was some nutty *Real World* groupie. This whole story about being scared that people

MALO: WHO'S A BETTER KISSER, TECK OR RUTHIE? OH MY GOD! I CAN'T SAY. IT'S DIFFERENT. HE'S A GUY AND SHE'S A GIRL. WHAT I HAVE WITH TECK IS ANIMAL ATTRACTION, BUT WITH RUTHIE IT'S LOVE.

nothing I could do could change what had happened. And I just let go. I actually wanted to give her a big kiss good-bye at the airport, but I chickened out. Still, I'm ready to face the truth and deal with the reality of what my love for Ruthie means. The show wasn't the most important part of my life. Ruthie was.

After Ruthie left Hawaii, and she got back to New Jersey, we talked every day. I came out to visit her. It's not dramatic anymore. Maybe that's because there are no roommates around. It's really nice and romantic. But I'm still bitter. *The Real*

are going to think she's a lesbian? What the hell is that? That's fiction. She kissed Ruthie on camera a million times. That was not her problem. Her problem was that she was wavering between Ruthie and Teck. She freaked out about the camera because she was taking crap from the house and Ruthie ditched her. I thought she was a big step down from Jess. "Ruthie," I said, "you can do better."

Ruthie: I realize now that I was completely unfair to Malo. The roommates were quick not to trust people, and I went along with it.

Kaia & Matt

COLIN: Near the end of our time in Hawaii, Kaia wanted to do the wild monkey dance with Matt. She also says she fell in love with him. What? Kaia told me Matt wasn't up to doing the horizontal tango with her, but they did kiss. Matt said so too. I was like, "Damn, just think, she kissed Ruthie."

Amaya: I think Kaia and Matt are a very fitting couple. I think it's just all for the cameras. It has to be. I saw Matt rubbing Kaia's back once. The setup, it just looked contrived. Not like what happened between me and Colin, which was real. Why play with that kind of emotion? It's like a bad *Jerry Springer* episode.

Ruthie: I think Kaia wants what she can't have, and that what motivates her is how much Matt's in like with my sister Sara. I think that Matt values his and Kaia's friendship, but he was caught off guard by her feelings for him. There's a tendency for someone to like back someone when they like you.

Matt: Kaia and I ended the show with a strange dynamic. I don't think it's a very comfortable thing when friends explore their feelings for each other, and one of them decides not to go with it. I kept telling her I considered her a deep friend, but not a girlfriend. She didn't want to hear it. I kept telling her all I can think about is Sara. She didn't want to hear that, either. Her logic was: *I'm here. She's not. Pick me.* She kept saying we need closure. Well, I had closure. It was very clear to me that there was not going to be a relationship between us.

She's very sexy. She fully seduced me. How did she do it? Well, she did a lot of bad-mouthing of Sara, calling into question my attraction to someone she says I don't know. And she very much encouraged my consumption of adult beverages.

So, on one of the last nights, we were lying in her bed. I'm still trying to talk about Sara. But she's trying to get us to kiss. The cameras were above us, and she kept saying to me, "Look, if we give them a shot of us kissing, they'll leave us alone." But I didn't want to be left alone! I had no reason to be left alone!

Kaia: I feel like I want to keep in touch with Matt for the rest of my life. I wrote him a poem expressing how I felt. I don't know if he was ready to hear all that. I don't think he was. He said to me, "I don't know how fleeting your feelings are." That assures me he wasn't ready.

I think he cares about me a lot. I think he's definitely attracted to me, but I don't know if he knows what he wants from me. I am open to a relationship with Matt. It'd be nice. In fact, I'd love that. If it's meant to happen, it will. As for Sara, I'm not personally involved in their relationship so I can't comment on it. I'm interested in talking about me.

Matt and I kissed a few times during the last week in Hawaii. Our first kiss was during the variety show. I felt nervous about kissing him, for the variety show, because I really wanted to. It was sensual. I told Matt about the love I was feeling toward him. Telling him how I felt was a way of saying thank you. He's taught me a lot about myself.

The last day of the show, we had horrible communication. Here I'd laid my feelings on the table. I expected him to come to me and he didn't. I think we were both feeling the pressure of the cameras going off. Like: "Oh, my God, do we have to end this drama for TV land?"

We didn't talk until the show ended, though in my eyes there still was no real closure. I don't think he's comfortable telling me how he feels. I'm definitely going to visit him in L.A., but I don't know if we'll ever have any completion. Am I scared of being rejected? No. You'll never lose if you express yourself. This process has taught me I have nothing to fear. Being rejected and losing are a natural process.

THE AFTERMATH

Matt: Kaia came to visit me after the show. She just showed up out of the blue, called me from LAX and told me to pick her up. She was like, "Can I crash at your place? I don't have a flight until the morning." She came to my house, and immediately I realized she had no intention of leaving. Ever.

On the third day, she asked me if she could sleep in my bed. I told her it would make me uncomfortable. She told me she thought that my rejection of her in Hawaii had to do with the fact that I didn't want to engage in things with her in front of the camera. I told her no. I'm not interested. I'm really sorry.

She still didn't leave. She was just lounging around, making phone calls, eating my food. She brought this tension into my house, and it was disgusting. I'd spurned her advances, and she kept telling me how she'd never been rejected by a man before. It made our conversations incredibly uncomfortable.

I felt like I had to take care of her, but I had stuff to do—meetings to go to and buddies to be with. I told her in a very sweet way she had to leave. She was there a week.

We've corresponded since, and I've told her that I'm sorry I didn't treat her well. But, honestly, she really was kind of rude. She literally had clothes all over the house. In Hawaii, I used to think she was a really confident person. Ruthie and Amaya had both told me she was selfish. But I thought, *No, she's just confident.* But, she came out here, and for the first time I realized Kaia is self-important, not self-confident.

My housemates were pretty shocked. They were like, "That girl wants to sleep in your room and you don't want her." They couldn't believe I'd remove someone from our house. Socially, I've always been a put-on-a-happy-face guy. Perhaps this is a renewed sense of strength.

Kaia: I think towards the end of our time in Hawaii our emotions were really raw. I think that's one of the reasons I developed feelings for Matt. I think another part of it was that he really wasn't who I thought he was. It was like I created somebody that I wanted him to be, that I think he has the potential to be, but who he isn't. I think he's the kind of person who caters to whomever he's talking. If I think about anybody who was the most business-like, it was Matt. He was concerned about how he came off, and I think that's why he tried to get close to me. He wanted to play a role, and somehow I figured into it. Our time in LA was really weird. He was very silent the whole time. I ended up hanging out with his roommates a lot. He wasn't rude. He was just caught up in stuff. I decided to leave early in order to respect his space. I hear he's saying he kicked me out, but it couldn't be further from the truth. He had every opportunity to tell me he wanted to be alone, and he never used it.

RUTHIE: I LET ALCOHOL TAKE OVER MY LIFE. I DIDN'T DO IT ON PURPOSE; IT'S JUST SOMETHING THAT HAPPENED.

Drinking

RUTHiE: I don't think I have a drinking problem, but people will think I do. And I know people are going to think it's my past that made me drink. That's such bulls**t. You can learn from your past, but you can't blame it. It wasn't my upbringing that put me in an alcoholic state. I just got out of control.

When I was at school, I had two internships and I was getting good grades, going to classes all the time. I was an example to my friends because I

I still drink once in a while, but drinking actually makes me tired. It's not as hype as it seemed to be. God, what an idiot I was. What can I say? You live, you learn, you move on. I strive to be so positive. I want people to know that there are many different sides of me: I'm fun to be around; I'm a daredevil; I can be relaxed and philosophical. There's so much more to me than the drinking. I hope viewers will see that as well.

KAIA: WE WENT INTO OUR SEASON WITH A BANG. ALCOHOL POISONING ON THE SECOND DAY? IT WASN'T EXACTLY EASY TO BOUNCE BACK.

would party just as hard as I studied. When I got to Hawaii, partying stopped being a reward for hard work; it became the priority and the escape. I needed to escape from everything that was happening with my family, and the process.

I feel more relaxed when I'm drunk. Then again, I'm already uninhibited. People drink so that they can get to where I am when I'm sober. So, when I'm drunk, it's just even more. When I drink, it's too much for society. Drinking does not help me communicate with people, that's for sure. The only reason I drank in front of my roommates was because they told me not to. I acted like a little rebel. I was irresponsible. I never thought about drinking. I just did it. The more my roommates told me not to, the more I drank. I was like, "f**k it, f**k it, f**k it," that's all I could think. Just f**k it. I can analyze the whole situation 200 different ways, and I still don't know why I overdid it. Of course, it was a big mistake.

COLiN: Ruthie has never acknowledged a problem. Yes, in my opinion, she has a drinking problem. And, yes, her future scares me.

AMaya: Ruthie is an inspiration. But I had a hard time finding inspiration in her when she drank. She's very sparkly, but I admit I was scared off by her when she was drinking.

TECK: I think Ruthie's the type of person who goes overboard when she drinks. She didn't drink every day. But when she did drink, she was looking like an idiot.

One night, we got into a huge fight. It was late and Ruthie said she was hot. She was drunk, of course, and decided she wanted to walk on the pier. Fine, okay, I'll do that. But then this dumb broad wants to jump off the pier. I said no way. It was dark and she was drunk. We were actually physically fighting, and I had to restrain her.

The Lapdance

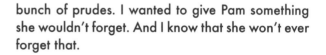

RUTHIE: I lapdance when I'm sober. And let me set the record straight, I only had two drinks before I gave that lapdance to Pam. I was buzzed, but not drunk. If I was too drunk, I don't think I could have stood on that table. Also, it was totally premeditated. I'd already told Calvin I was going to do it. I guess he just didn't realize what it would actually be. I'm not the kind of person to give a card. I give birthday wishes the Ruthie way. It was supposed to be *Hahahaha, that's funny.* In New York, you'd laugh that off. But in Hawaii, it was a big deal. Pam should have just laughed it off.

I've done lapdances a million times. That was the first time I'd gotten the reaction of, *What the hell?* I wasn't in my element. I was in conservative Hawaii. I should have known better. I was with a bunch of prudes. I wanted to give Pam something she wouldn't forget. And I know that she won't ever forget that.

PAM: Ruthie's lapdance? Well, I was shocked. What I was expecting was a cake. Ruthie and I were sitting down, having a nice conversation. Amaya came over and was urging me onto the dance floor. Ruthie stopped us, saying, "Wait, I wanna give you something." And that's when the lapdance happened. By Ruthie's standards, I know it wasn't raunchy. But, me, I've never been in that position and it was so surprising. Ruthie lifted up her shirt and showed me her boobs; she was moving her a** in my face.

I was never mad at her. But I didn't know how to act after that. I live here in Hawaii. I go to that club. I was embarrassed. That's not a normal thing for that club. Why did she do it? When I finally talked to her about it, she told me she thought it was funny, and we just had to relax. Sometimes the stuff that Ruthie does just for fun intrudes on people's comfort levels. But I'm easygoing enough to know it was just Ruthie being Ruthie.

JON MURRAY, creator: Since Ruthie doesn't remember much of her alcohol-induced behavior, I am interested in talking to her after she's seen all the shows. Hopefully seeing what she was like when she was drunk will have a sobering effect on her.

PAM, RUTHIE & CALVIN

The First Ultimatum

Matt Kunitz, Supervising Producer: Mary-Ellis, Jon, and I came to an early realization that Ruthie's drinking was jeopardizing herself and others. After the second day of the show, when the incident happened with the alcohol poisoning, we went and got expert advice about how to handle a cast member who abuses alcohol. We were monitoring the situation. Then, an incident happened with drunk driving. That really pushed us to intervene. We needed to make sure Ruthie and her roommates were as safe as possible. We could no longer not be involved.

I don't like being on camera. I'm a behind-the-scenes person. If it were up to me, I would not have talked to Ruthie on-camera, but because my intervention would have a major effect on her life, I had no choice. Why did we decide to give the ultimatum? Well, our experts told us you can't just tell her she's not allowed to drink. It wouldn't work. So, we told Ruthie she had to see an addiction counselor two or three times a week. But then the glass incident happened....

Ruthie: It was the day after I drove drunk, 90 miles an hour in a friend's BMW, that I first got in trouble. I was swerving all around, trying to get away from the crew. I knew I was going to be in deep s**t. The next day, when I was asked to meet the producer, I didn't realize that the cameras were also going to be there. But, when I got to the park, there they were. I'd seen the Seattle season. I knew when the producers made an appearance, it was trouble. But, I was still on my rampage then. I wasn't about to do a 180. I wasn't going to change until I was ready.

THE GLASS

Colin: I guess you could say the glass incident was the straw that broke the camel's back. Teck's yelling woke me up. He was going off like crazy. Well, there I am, peeking my head through the curtain of my bedroom, sort of disbelieving. Then, Teck said this thing that cracked me up completely. He started screaming at Ruthie: "What if we had company?" I just lost it. He must have been at a loss for something to say. All of a sudden, at the heat of the moment, he turned into a 1950s housewife. This is a guy who goes on a date to McDonald's or Burger King. Company? He never had company—at least not like that!

Teck: That night that Ruthie broke the glass, I was pissed. That is just not how you behave. I'd been dealing with her all night, and practically had to carry her home. When I was first screaming at her, I was really screaming at her. Then, I went back into my room and recollected myself. When I came back, yeah, I was putting it on a bit for the cameras. But I wasn't saying anything I didn't mean.

The Second Ultimatum

Ruthie: It was pretty ironic that I got kicked out when I did. The thing is I had already decided to change my behavior. That's what nobody understood. If you don't want to change, you can't. Well, I decided I wanted to change a week before I was kicked out. A lot of things had affected me—visiting my foster family, seeing my dad, having my sisters in town. I was ready to change my ways, but it was too late.

My roommates lied to me. They were sneaking around. They didn't trust me. No one had enough balls to approach me. They were panicking. If I had to guess, it was Amaya and Justin who pushed my getting kicked out the most. Amaya thinks she knows everything about alcoholism and Justin can be really logical and emotionless. And Matt, he told me he would be on my side, that he was the only one who supported me and was against the ultimatum. Then, on the day of the meeting, he was the one reading from the notebook. When he started reading, I felt like I'd lost all the air inside of me.

At least my college friends were there. That was

Sara & Ruthie

a blessing. They reminded me how strong I was.

Kaia: Even if Ruthie's drinking problem was only a phase, it was not a healthy one. The whole intervention was so hard for me. I did long confessionals about it. I felt very pressured to make a quick decision. In retrospect, I don't know why we made such a quick decision, except that her drinking was truly affecting all of our lives. At the time, I felt Ruthie was in no position to see it from our perspectives. But it was only care that motivated me. I can't say the same for Amaya. Many times, after Ruthie left, she mentioned that she didn't want her to come back. Very telling.

Amaya: The intervention would have worked better if Matt hadn't told Ruthie about it beforehand. Also, I think the production people could have been more involved during the intervention. If they could have come in for Irene and Stephen's slap, they should have helped more with us. It was really difficult.

Sara (Ruthie's Sister): The whole thing went so fast. I didn't have time to think about what I thought or whether Ruthie had a drinking problem. All I could do was try to get the roommates to give Ruthie a chance. And in the end, I feel like I didn't get to do that.

It was so shocking to me that Ruthie would get kicked out. That's not the kind of Ruthie I know. She has more best friends than anyone. She wasn't herself on the show. I think she was intimidated by Teck. He was the friendly one, the center of attention. That's usually her.

Ruthie: If people think my story is compelling just from what they see on the show, well, that's funny; they don't know the half of it. Right before I was kicked out, all of this stuff was stressing me out.

Here's a list of what was bothering me:

1. Right before I came to Hawaii, there was an incident at school. I passed out after a party, fell asleep, and woke up to find a guy in my bed who was touching me. I started screaming, and he got out—but I had no idea whether I'd been assaulted or not. That was being investigated when I got to the show. Scary, right?

2. I was upset about getting alcohol poisoning on the second day.

3. I was upset that Jess was gone.

4. My family: There was stuff going on with my dad, with my twin sister Sara, with my mom and her family. I can't talk about any of it, really. Let's just say there couldn't have been any more going on in my life when all that drinking was happening. That's not an excuse, but it's true.

MATT'S ROLE

Matt: I feel I played a profound role in helping Ruthie better her situation. You never know your character's strength until it's tested. I look at my behavior during the week of the intervention, and I think: *You were selfless.* I did not think about myself once that week. I put my life on hold in order to devote myself solely to someone in need. It takes a lot of strength to stand up for the person being picked on.

When everyone wanted Ruthie to move out of the house, I was there for her. I was spending day and night with her and her sisters; I

was a man under pressure. I did whatever I needed to do to save Ruthie's soul. When we called the house meeting, Ruthie came to me in tears and challenged me. She really wanted to know what it was about. She asked me straight up to tell her what it was about. Well, what was I supposed to do? Twenty hours earlier, she'd almost jumped off a hotel terrace. I stayed true to myself. I couldn't in good conscience lie to her. I think only tragedy would have come from it. So, no, I didn't sell out my roommates. I thought the meeting was about supporting Ruthie. I had Ruthie's best interests at heart. Not mine. But, I do think intervention was the right thing to do. Ruthie told me time and again that if we'd given her a "F**k up again and you're out" clause, she would have f**ked up again.

The intervention specialist said the ultimatum had to be delivered by me because of my rapport with Ruthie. Really, I tried to weasel out of it. I didn't want to give it. But, I don't regret giving the ultimatum, because it went well. And look what happened? It worked. To the best of my knowledge, Ruthie's not drinking. That's a success story.

Leaving

RUTHIE: IT WAS WEIRD TO LEAVE. IMAGINE HOW I FELT WHEN THE AUDIO PERSON DE-MIKED ME IN THE DRIVEWAY. LEAVING WAS LIKE A DEEP SIGH. I DIDN'T THINK I WAS GONNA COME BACK TO THE HOUSE. <u>THIS IS IT, I THOUGHT. IT'S DONE.</u>

At that point, I really didn't care about coming back. I was thinking, *My story, it's going to get finished on or off camera. Just because I'm getting kicked off the show, doesn't mean my life is over.* The whole thing was a revolution. Was I thinking about other *Real World*—ers who'd been kicked off? No. I don't think I have anything in common with them.

I knew I wouldn't miss my roommates when I was away. The only ones I thought I'd miss were the crew members. They saw me through everything. They saw the good, the bad, the sober. The only validation I had at the time was the sense that the crew still liked me. They couldn't actually express that, they couldn't give me advice, but I felt it anyway.

Right after I left the house, I dropped off my stuff in storage. Then I went to the hotel where my sisters were staying. I wasn't thinking about enrolling in the program. I couldn't just yet. I needed to get my bearings, to regain my sanity. It felt like such a relief to be out of the house. It was such an uninviting place at the time. I couldn't decide whether to go to the program, but after much talk with my sister and friends, I decided to go.

THE PROGRAM

I went to the program. It was like living in an apartment or a dorm with a bunch of other women. I even got in trouble when I was there. I'd decided not to drink. I wasn't having cravings. So, there I was, just trying to have fun. I became the program's in-house advocate for fun and sobriety. I was not going to sit back and be quiet. The other women were like, "You're too much. Stop dancing to the radio. If you relax, you'll get out of here." I just couldn't do it. So, of course, my counselor had to take me aside and reprimand me for being the little rebel once again. As I said, I'm wild even when I don't drink.

It wasn't like the place was jail or anything. I got passes to leave all the time. I'd go to the beach or to see friends. All in all, the time was well-spent. I found out what I needed to know. What I learned in the program is that nobody can tell you if you have a drinking problem, only you can tell yourself. Nobody can tell you not to drink or to drink. You have to decide for yourself.

It would be ideal not to drink again, but nobody knows what is going to happen.

Coming Back

RUTHIE: IT HAD NOTHING TO DO WITH GETTING BACK INTO THE HOUSE. I JUST WANTED TO FIND OUT IF I WAS AN ALCOHOLIC OR NOT.

RUTHIE: Wanna know one of the reasons I came back? Because I want people out there to know that you can come from s**t and go through s**t and mess up your life. But you can turn around and change and inspire people.

So I came back. Amaya told me she couldn't understand why I was as happy as I was. She thought that after the break, I should have questioned my roommates. She thought I should have gotten into it with them. What she didn't understand was at that point I couldn't care less.

Matt and Colin, they were the only ones whose motives I ever questioned. Colin, because I feel like he's more real than the others and I actually cared what he thought. And Matt, because I felt like he'd stabbed me in the back. Then again, he was the only roommate who tried to contact me when I was gone. But, whatever, it really doesn't matter. If you have a good heart, it'll definitely shine through no matter what.

AMAYA: I was very, very uncomfortable having Ruthie back in the house. I've encountered a lot of alcoholism in my life. If I sound insensitive, I'm sorry. But I had two friends who were killed because of alcohol, and I have another friend who's in a downward spiral. It's been a very hard thing in my life seeing this type of destruction. So I distance myself from people with drinking problems.

COLIN: Ruthie did stop drinking for two months, which is an accomplishment. But she'll only say, "I will stop drinking for two months," and nothing more. I think that's weak.

TECK: When Ruthie came back to the house, we never had a real conversation. We never sat down and talked about how things were different. I regret that. People might think that Ruthie and I didn't like each other, but I'm a big fan. I really am. I'd love to be able to call Ruthie and be like, "Whoa, what's up, Ruthie?" But I don't know if I could. I was never mad at her once she got back—skeptical, I admit—but not mad. She has some ill feelings toward me, but once she sees the episodes she'll know who was looking after her. There was a lot of bulls**t conversations happening that I wasn't a part of.

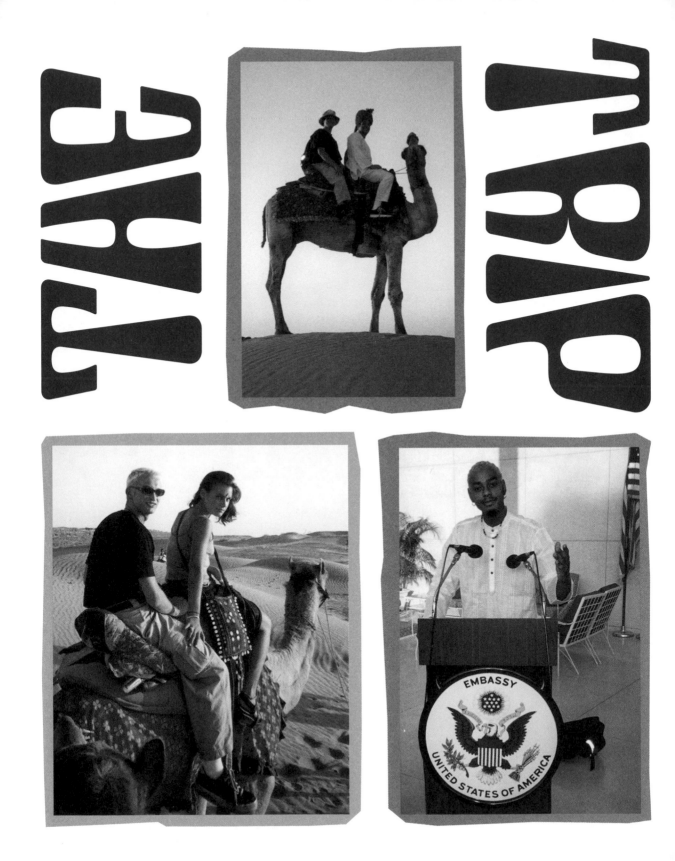

THE TRAP

TECK: INDIA WAS NOT ABOUT TECK BEING WILD AND CRAZY. IT WAS ABOUT TECUMSHEA LEARNING ABOUT THE PEOPLE IN INDIA. IN INDIA, I REMOVED MYSELF FROM MY ROOMMATES. I DIDN'T WANT ANYONE TO PUT HIS POINT OF VIEW ON ME.

AMAYA: WHEN I THINK OF INDIA, I THINK OF COWS IN THE STREETS, MONKEYS JUST ROAMING ABOUT. I THINK OF SMALL CHILDREN BEGGING. I THINK OF BRIGHTLY COLORED SARIS AGAINST A VERY PALE, DRAB EXISTENCE. INDIA IS VERY HARD TO DESCRIBE IN WORDS.

THE BODIES

Nudity

TECK: I'm the one who started it. My boys at home were like, "I know you. I know you're going to jump in the pool naked on the first day." I had to do it for them. Since I brought it on, it's all good with me. The more ass, the better. There's nothing wrong with the human body.

AMAYA: All that nudity was not neccessary. We don't live in a colony. Not to sound too Christian, but your body is a gift, and I'd rather show it to someone I care about. Down the beach from us there was a nude beach where big-butted men had their dingleberries out. Why couldn't they all have just gone there?

RUTHIE: There's a certain freedom to being naked, it's no big deal. At my apartment at Rutgers, I'd walk around naked all the time. You're supposed to be yourself on *The Real World*, so that's what I did. I'd forgotten that the crew was watching everything. Then, it kind of hit me: "Oh my God, the poor crew, they watched me like this all the time." If I

attracted to her? No. I'd lost my attraction to her a long time before that.

COLIN: I didn't need any of the nudity. Kaia's breasts, I didn't need to see. And not only that, she doesn't wear underwear. One time, I was playing pool, and I looked up—she was sitting on a stool, wearing a skirt—and I was like, "Uh, Kaia, I'm seeing something that belongs to you." Teck's package was completely unnecessary, I will die a happy man if I never see his d**k again. No, I do not think taking my shirt off is the equivalent. It was hot!

JUSTIN: The nudity? It's not how I live, but no big deal. Really, it is beneath comment.

Matt: I appreciated the nudity. Those who took off their clothes had nothing to hide.

Matt KUNitZ, SUPERViSING PRODUCER: For production, the nudity was a nightmare. The machine to blur their bodies costs about $150 per nipple. Plus, we had nowhere to put their mikes. We had to cre-

> **KAIA:** I THINK THIS CAST IS REALLY BEAUTIFUL. I DON'T THINK I'LL EVER GET SICK OF LOOKING AT US. FRANKLY, I THINK THE WHOLE NUDITY THING IS A NON-ISSUE.

were them, I'd be like, "Ruthie, put your clothes back on." I was naked on the treadmill, when I mopped the floor, everywhere. Colin told me that when I was gone, Kaia didn't get naked at all. It was just when I was there.

Anyway, except for one time that I know about, Kaia never was completely naked. Usually, she was just topless. She was only bottomless once. That was when we were hanging out—me, Malo, and this other friend of Kaia's. We were doing these nude photos out by the volcano. She still had her bottoms on, and the pictures were looking funny. So, I was like, "Hey, can you take them off?" So, she did. Yeah, we hugged naked and stuff. But, was

ate a new kind of mike that we hid in a necklace. Then they'd walk down the beach naked. Of course, by the end of the season the camera people had come up with many creative ways of hiding body parts. But it's difficult when you've got three naked girls baby-oiling themselves down on the hammock, completely nude. You've definitely got to go for some weird angles.

JON MURRAY, CREATOR: Was nudity a factor in *The Real World—Hawaii's* astronomical ratings? Absolutely, but it only got viewers in the door. It was the powerful stories, like Ruthie's battle with alcohol and the Colin/Amaya relationship, that kept them coming back.

Body Image

Teck: I don't have the biggest chest or the biggest legs. I may have the biggest johnson, but other than that, I have a little puny body. I'm not ashamed of it. I love my body. I love myself. I am the man.

Matt: I have a lot of insecurities about my physical appearance. And you know what? Living with six beautiful people only magnified them. When I was growing up, I had a baby-sitter who helped raise me and who would call me fat. She'd tell me I was getting fat and not as cute as I used to be. So perhaps that has something to do with it.

Amaya: When you're different in any way, you get picked on. As the earliest developer of my friends, I know this. And it wasn't only in school that I was picked on because of my body. I was eleven and riding on a subway in Oakland in a little-girl dress with my t*ts hanging out. Some guy, old enough to be my father, grabbed my ass. It was very traumatizing.

From junior high to sophomore year of high school, I wore big baggy clothes—T-shirts and jeans and overalls. It took me so long to get comfortable with my body. I actually played a stripper in a school play, and started getting asked out by all these guys. When I started wearing clothes my size, people were like, "Whoa, you lost all this weight." I was like, "No, I'm just getting comfortable with my body."

Freshman year of college, I gained twelve pounds. That's the year I started throwing up. I was in Los Angeles where everyone looks a certain way. Not to mention that college is a breeding ground for eating disorders. For about six months, I'd throw up twice a day. I never did the laxative thing. I'd just eat these massive meals at the dorm then go and throw them up. I think I hid it very well. My parents didn't even know.

My mom was very distressed when she found out. But I'm stubborn that way. I want to deal with things on my own. I moved past bulimia on my own. I knew what I was doing was wrong and I realized it was going to hurt me too much in my life. I didn't want to damage my internal organs. So, you know what I did? I started writing letters to myself for inspiration. I got back to the weight I am now, which is probably 113 pounds. (Remember, my boobs alone probably weigh seven or eight pounds.) I love to eat food. I live on a steady diet of buffalo wings and pizza. And I'm proud of my pooch. I don't get any complaints about it. I know guys like it.

But I do have a nervous stomach. I'm even more embarrassed about that than the bulimia. When there's stress, I lose my appetite and I barf. I'd go

to school dances, and I'd get so nervous I'd have to leave and throw up. And at one point, after breaking up with a boyfriend, I couldn't eat for a month. The only thing I could consume was tea. I was thinner than I'd ever been. A size 2 was falling off me. Honestly, I thought I looked disgusting.

I hate that anxiety over a man stopped me from eating. It's so embarrassing, but a movie that showed me the error of my ways was *The First Wives Club*. Even if people think it's silly, it sends a good message: You don't need a man in your life as long as you're strong.

Unfortunately, I did continue to throw up on *The Real World*. I guess you could even say I threw up often, although I never threw up meals—just water. I was just nervous all the time. In his inimitable way, Matt once tried to get me to say I was bulimic on camera. But that's really not an issue any more.

As for my body image, well, the fact that I wore a bikini on camera just proves to me that I've gotten more okay with my body. Kaia's confidence in her looks? Good for her. But there's confidence and then there's arrogance. She told me, "Amaya, you're very pretty and pretty girls are always intimidated by me, because I'm so beautiful." I was like, that's not the reason I'm intimidated by you.

Kaia: I've always been perceived as being confident about my looks, but it was when I was thirteen, I learned to love how I looked. It was a necessity for me. I would come home from school and tell my mom how my body was different from other peo-

ple's. She would tell me that the difference was beautiful. So, that's what I learned to think, and that's how I behaved. Now, I can be comfortable physically at all times.

In high school, I was a bad girl. My friends and I thought we were the s**t. We called ourselves "The Five Most Wanted." So I guess I've carried myself with this confidence for a while.

Amaya puking was pretty distressing. I heard it, knew she was doing it and I knew she wasn't happy with her body. From the get-go, I was telling her she was gorgeous. She was just really insecure. As for Ruthie, there was a time when I was sure she was seeking out the wrong kind of attention for her body. She'd take her clothes off for shock value.

Baywatch

Ruthie: When I was in Hawaii, I auditioned for *Baywatch*. I think other members of the cast did, too, but I'm the only one who got called back. It was when I was off the show. I got a pass to leave the center for a whole day. There were more than 1,000 applicants, but just seventy-five made the initial cut. I was one of them. They don't care who you are. They just look at you. I had to wear a bathing suit, and turn around for them so they could see me from all angles. I don't think I'm *Baywatch* material, but it was fun.

THE WORK

Local Motion

TECK: Local Motion was the bomb. It was easy, but I still felt like I was working. I did a lot of promoting and public relations. I was the mouthpiece. I also did a lot of legwork, flyer-ing, going to radio stations. I was involved in every aspect of the job. I worked the hardest, hell yeah.

COLIN: Teck worked the hardest? That's a joke. When Teck got into work early the second day, it's because he slept in some girl's apartment near Local Motion. It's bulls**t that he worked the most. I don't consider talking to your friends doing PR. I think that's what he considered work.

Local Motion was cool, but I wish we had worked at a TV station. That would have really been awesome.

KAIA: Local Motion was very urban, very Hawaiian. In the beginning, I was really excited about the job. We saw a lot of really good talent. It's a small music scene in Hawaii, and we were basically asked to jump-start it. I was most excited about the work when I was onstage. That was my idea originally, that we should go onstage.

AMAYA: While working at Local Motion, I had more money than I ever did in my life. I really liked the cafe. I don't drink coffee, but I like making it. Plus, I got to talk to so many people—tourists and locals.

RUTHIE: Calvin was a big part of my time here. He was one of the best bosses that I've had. I really feel that the performance space was meant for us because all of us roommates have a lot of talents and creativity. It's cool that in the end we did perform, but we could've done more.

VOLUNTEERING

BIG BROTHERS

Matt: Working for Big Brothers, Big Sisters was the most rewarding aspect of my *Real World–Hawaii* experience. Every Tuesday for fifteen weeks, I volunteered my time for three hours at Kalihiwaena elementary school. My little brother's name was George, a tough-as-nails 9-year-old Samoan kid.

George and I got along famously. He's a great kid who made tremendous strides with his math and reading skills under my tutelage.

THE MARRIAGE PROJECT

JUSTIN: In Hawaii, I was engaged in several initiatives at The Marriage Project. I did some expressly legal work; I did some lobbying and legislative watchdog stuff; I beefed up the group's Web resources; I did some direct-action organizing for the NGLT-funded (National Gay & Lesbian Task Force) "equality begins at home" rally for the state of Hawaii. All in all, it was a fantastic time. I met some great, dedicated people.

The Spirit of Aloha

CALVIN: I WOULD SAY THE CAST DEFINITELY ADAPTED TO THE SPIRIT OF ALOHA. THEY ALL TOOK IT ON, AND I HOPE THEY LEFT WITH IT IN THEIR HEARTS.

For me, the main goal was to share with the cast the spirit of Aloha. What is the spirit of Aloha? It's how we describe the way all the different cultures live harmoniously here in Hawaii. Hawaii is a melting pot for so many different people of different ethnic backgrounds. We need to be open to different cultures. We need to be generous.

I guess you could say the job was easy. I tried to make it as fun as possible. How would I rate them? Well...

Justin is a bright guy, but he was always someplace else. I tried to motivate him, but his concerns were really more global.

Matt was very enthusiastic, especially when it came to promotions.

Teck is the high-energy guy. His heart was on the stage. Yes, I do believe he was one of the hardest workers.

Colin also took initiative to promote the shows.

Ruthie, I guess she had a lot of personal issues.

PaM, Matt & CalViN

There was a time when she wasn't proud of her Hawaiian heritage. She almost lost her Aloha spirit. But I took her out alone and we had a long talk about appreciating your island roots.

Kaia's energy and enthusiasm would go in and out. She'd get really motivated and then drop it. Making coffee was good for her, but dealing with the customers wasn't.

Amaya reminded me of a princess, always bubbly and happy. She and my girlfriend Pam got along because they both came from really nice families. She's very warm with a lot of heart, kind of motherly.

I'm nervous about how Hawaii is going to be portrayed. It will bother me if I don't see the cast carrying on with the spirit of Aloha. I don't know how they behaved when they weren't with me. I do know that when they were working, their personalities shone.

The Variety Show

Amaya: During the variety show, I saw who Matt really was. He'd subtly insult Ruthie or look at me in a weird, angry, calculated, disappointed way. There was some total showboating going on.

Matt: Ten minutes after the variety show ended, it hit me big-time: we pulled it off. It went so smooth. I felt like pounding my chest because I had a great deal of pride for the way the show went off. It was a fitting way to end our stint at Local Motion.

> Excerpt from **"Hired Lover"** by Matt
> Starring: Kaia as Sabrina and Matt as Micky
>
> *Sabrina and Micky lock eyes. She moves toward him in a seductive manner...*
>
> SABRINA: I have been waiting for that kiss good-night for five years...
>
> MICKY: I know....
>
> *Sabrina runs her fingers through Micky's hair and kisses him big-time on the mouth...*
>
> SABRINA: Don't worry, Micky. You will never have to worry about Don Genovese again.
>
> MICKY: Thank you, Sabrina.
>
> SABRINA: Everything's gonna be all right.
>
> MICKY: Thank you. Thank you so much.
>
> BLACK OUT
>
> GUN SHOT
>
> *(fade out)*

During the skit, I enjoyed kissing Kaia. I will be honest about that. She has very soft lips. I've kissed enough lips in my time—Ruthie's and Amaya's included—to know that there are soft lips and there are not-so-soft lips. And Kaia's lips are very soft and alluring, and it's enjoyable. This definitely wasn't a stage kiss. It was a big-time, passionate, tongue-jabbing kiss on the mouth. That is not a stage kiss.

> **"Blue"** *by Kaia*
>
> What is it that attracts me to you?
> Oh blue it is finally true.
> Not fleeting love which I describe myself to find
> in nooks and crannies of life.
> A consistent ever growing
> desire
> to hold you and be held by you.
> I never imagined not to look but to find
> the ever expanding lust for your touch.
>
> A bright green terry cloth shirt
> brightening the room again and again and
> again.
> Never ending torrents
> When others barely trickle
> My feet tingle
> A sparkling giggle
> Ever widening smiles
> Soft flow like tears free to express emotion
> Which surrounds others confidently.
> Oh Blue. It is you.

As Kaia read that poem, my heart was racing. I felt touched by her words and by her gesture. It's one thing to take me aside in private and tell me how much she loves me, but it's another thing to announce it to the audience, that she likes me, under the moniker Blue, which is apropos because of my glasses. And because of the shirts I wear. Blue is my color.

"Introduction to Variety Show" *by Ruthie*

This is the Real, "WHAT?!"
Real lives, Realize, our eyes visualize, we gotsta revolutionize
the prize
To our demise the present presents WE RISE
And if we dare paint the disguise with lies, we die
Up the creek we seek to display the stars
Dump the bands dump the flyers, dump the m'f bars
We had all this to say, now I'm saying it
It's time to stop talking about the game and start
Playing it
I was waiting inspiration, calculation ain't correct
What's the deal, get the Real 7 strangers to connect
No need to settle, stop the meddle
It's resurrection of the heart

Perceptions need corrections
So this day is just a start
There was once was a thing called Trust
In my mind, it only exists
reciprocal to my Self, a must
Who is to risk again and again
And still win in the journey
In the End
For the End is near to us
For those we hold dear to us
Stand up in the back of the bus
It's time to take the stage, stop the mackin' and the fuss
At first, instant strangers
Instant Friends?!
And these "Friends," he, she, THEM
Are by no means, Means
and Means to an End
We live, we work, we laugh, we cry
Misunderstanding along with wondering WHY?
Kicked out onto the street to a place Unknown
Was I not Worthy?
From what I have shown?
And yet the script won't ever change
7 strangers, 7 friends, friends so strange
In suspended Reality we call "Real"
The one thing we cannot hide is the Truth we Feel
And love is lust, and lust is love
Pain is Rain and Rain spreads above
And beyond
But still we move on
And learn to ACCEPT
The Past is the Past
And we move One More Step
So without further due, I will step Aside
And present the 7 Strangers Performance with much, much, PRIDE

THE EXIT

JUSTIN: I KNOW EVERYONE THOUGHT I LEFT ONLY BECAUSE I WANTED TO DITCH THE SHOW. IT'S NOT TRUE. I APOLOGIZE IF I CAUSED ANYONE ANY GRIEF.

Leaving Early

JUSTIN: India was exhausting. When we got home, it felt like a lot of the flash of the whole experience had gone away. I was feeling restless. I missed my life. I was thinking, "I have a sweet life on the East Coast. What am I doing here?" It was partly that I was over the whole experience, and partly that I was just finished—ready to go.

But, in the end, those are not the reasons I left. My family was in crisis. That's why I left. My brother was visiting when we found out about illnesses in our family. It was incredibly troubling to me. I was my departure was Teck. He took people at face value, because he didn't care enough not to.

The whole thing was very unpleasant. I know the producers—or at least Matt Kunitz—thought that I shouldn't leave. But I felt I had to make a choice. I couldn't still be on the show and back with my family. I had to commit to one.

TECK: I think leaving was the best thing for Justin. He obviously wasn't happy. Early on, he mentioned to me that he might not last all four months.

RUTHIE: JUSTIN'S DEPARTURE WAS SO SUDDEN FOR ME. I WASN'T EVEN BACK YET. YOU COULD SEE IT IN HIS EYES THAT HE WASN'T HAPPY. IT'S TOO BAD, THOUGH. IT WOULD HAVE BEEN A GREAT VICTORY IF WE COULD HAVE ALL FINISHED THE SEASON TOGETHER.

truly distraught. I began to remove myself from the house. I didn't tell anybody what was going on, so in a sense I dug my own grave. There became a big gap between me and the people in the house. People got aggressively indifferent and standoffish with me. I had to figure out where my priorities lay. I could heal this situation in the house or be with my family at a crucial time. Obviously, we know which decision I made.

The person who was most understanding about

My advice was: Do whatever to make yourself happy. You're not in jail. If you're not happy, get yourself out. That's what I would do.

Matt: Justin told me there were members of his family that were terminally ill. If that happened to me, I'd be leaving too. When he was leaving, I think I helped Justin make his transition from Hawaii to home. He wanted to talk to everybody one-on-one, and I think I was the only one really there for him.

Staging an Exit

JUSTIN: When I didn't know what was happening with my family and I was just getting bored, Kaia and I started this dialogue about my departure. I told her I was thinking of leaving. For a day or so, she was telling me, "Don't go." But then, she was like, "Okay, do what you have to do but let's do it right."

I told her I'd do whatever she wanted, but we needed to be consistent. We talked about staging some story about how I'd impregnated her. It was pretty crazy. Did I take her seriously? Kind of. Really, it didn't much matter to me.

> I WAS THINKING: WHY NOT ATTEMPT TO STAGE SOME DRAMATIC DEPARTURE? BE ALL GUERRILLA! IT WOULD PROBABLY BOMB, BUT WHY NOT?

But then out of nowhere she came to me and told me it was not going to work. I was fine with that. I really didn't care. But then everything got—I don't know—incoherent. After we got back from India, she started distancing herself from me. I think she noticed how exclusive we seemed and for whatever reason she wanted to remedy it.

Kaia: Trying to stage story lines? As I saw it, Justin would always make comments about people's insecurities in the house and how he could prey upon them. It seemed to me he wanted to inflate things that were under the surface; he wanted to be a player behind the scenes. For instance, he wanted to get what he saw as Amaya's alleged eating disorder out into the open. I admit the way that we were talking about things was very insensitive.

As for his departure, he discussed with me certain stories that might be interesting, that might give him a reason for going other than being bored of the process and the roommates. I thought it was innocuous to make things up, but in the end I realized he needed to be on his own where leaving was concerned.

I don't know exactly what he was thinking, honestly. But he was definitely trying to instigate things. Anyone who knows me knows I wouldn't do that s**t.

Justin & Kaia

JUSTIN: I genuinely liked Kaia at first. I think she can be incredibly funny. I really don't understand what happened between us.

At first it was benign when I saw in Kaia the disjuncture between private/private and private, how she was with me and with everyone else. Honestly, I don't think anyone knows the half of what a bitch she was. She talked crap about everybody. I'm not saying I wasn't doing the same thing. I just wasn't as concerned about nipping and tucking.

After everything, it was mystifying to me that before I left, Kaia never asked me what was wrong.

I was pissed. I felt really hurt by Kaia at the end of my time in Hawaii. It doesn't make sense, because though I saw the negative aspects of her, I was also the one person who had a window into how awesome a person she is. I'm going to try to not let two weeks of confusion cloud that.

Kaia: I know being in the house was hard for Justin. If I had any agenda with him it was to get to know him. Originally becoming friends with him was my way of reaching out in order to say: "You definitely have something to offer to this process. What is

> **KAIA:** I THINK JUSTIN LEFT IN A VERY UNCOMFORTABLE WAY. THERE WAS A LOT OF DOUBT AS TO WHY HE ACTUALLY LEFT, BUT NO ONE REALLY CONFRONTED HIM. NO ONE WANTED HIM TO FEEL REJECTED. NOBODY COULD TALK TO HIM OPENLY—MYSELF INCLUDED.

It was clear she had some issue with me.

We went to the bank together, and I told her why I was going. She was like, "That sucks. I'm sorry." It was such a calculated, callous tone. Considering how much time we talked about her family....I was like *That's faithless.* I said, "I'm taking off soon and as my last pathetic gesture I would like to have a chat with you." It never happened. Just before I left, she gave me some pictures from India and a card that said something about trust.

it? Nobody sees it. Show it. If you have to show it through me, show it through me."

I think the game of the house for Justin had its moments of fun. But, given the amount of communication he had with people or attempted to have or cared about having, I think it makes sense that the whole thing lost its flavor pretty quickly for him. I for one think I made Justin uncomfortable when I probed into his personal life, when I asked questions about him.

AMaya: I don't know too much about Justin and Kaia's friendship, but they were joined at the hip. I'll never know what actually happened. Was the house better after Justin left? Yeah, it was more comfortable.

COLiN: I don't know what Justin and Kaia were saying to each other. They had conversations with each other I didn't understand at all. I think Justin's very insecure. Talking abstractly is a way of not saying what you mean. I'm all about saying what you mean. Kaia—we're just on different wavelengths. So, I don't really have any idea what went on between them at the end. You need subtitles to understand what they were saying. Together they are so confusing, I don't want to even begin to analyze their relationship—be it the beginning, the middle, or the end. I don't even think I want to know what the truth is with those two.

Matt: Kaia thought Justin was manipulating her, but I think there's a misconception there.

JON Murray, creator: Justin can be incredibly articulate and insightful about people, but forming friendships with people different from him seems to be hard for him. I don't think he ever really gave many of his fellow cast members a chance to develop a relationship with him. If he had, I think he would have had a lot more fun in Hawaii.

THE END

A House Divided

Confronting Amaya

AMAYA: I'VE NEVER BEEN DEPRESSED, BUT THAT LAST WEEK OF <u>THE REAL WORLD</u>, I WAS DEPRESSED. I WAS GOING TO SLEEP EARLY SO I WOULDN'T HAVE TO SEE MY ROOMMATES.

It was Matt and Kaia turning on me that really threw me. I gave Kaia a chance. I think she thought she wouldn't get enough screen time until she created some kind of drama, and that's why she turned against me. All the stuff she and Matt accused me of was so exaggerated. They were like: "You made us hate Colin." I was thinking, *I didn't make you feel d**k. In fact when you guys would tell me how Colin treated me badly, I'd stick up for him and say you didn't know him.*

With Kaia, I saw this person with a hard exterior. I thought there was a soft side underneath. Well, I was wrong. And, Matt, why is it any of his business what went on between me and Colin? He was always trying to insert himself in everybody's business. Just leave me alone. He slipped me a note at the airport, trying to apologize to me for being such a jerk the last week, but I couldn't deal with it.

As for Colin, well, yeah, he's kind of bounced to the Kaia and Matt side of the house. All I can say about that is that it's easy to prey on the wounded.

Matt: If Amaya were to step outside of herself and look back on her stay here, my guess is she would have to see a lot of her behavior as foolish. She needs to obtain some more character strength.

Throughout my time in Hawaii, I confronted Amaya. And each and every time my goal was to show her how she acted and get her to step outside herself and take a look at her behavior. And each and every time she acknowledged that I had a point. •

But, by our last week in Hawaii, I'd had enough with Amaya's behavior. She tried to seduce Colin's friend, Tony. What is that? And she's just always talking behind people's backs, exhibiting two-faced behavior. Colin was angry with her and Kaia was too. As the two of them started to get their feelings out into the open, I realized that I too had some grievances. The entire time in Hawaii, I'd been biting my tongue to err on the side of sensitivity. Even in India, when Justin and Kaia picked on her excessively, I tried to make her feel better. But, all of a sudden, I started realizing that Amaya had been taking me for granted. Many times, she would act like I didn't exist. She'd just walk past me, ignore me—me, her sole defender—in order to be nice to somebody else who'd been consistently cruel to her.

Why do I want to be so appreciated? All my life I've only been acknowledged for professional and scholastic achievements. I want to be recognized for more than that. As you help people walk through life, you hope they'll do the same for you. I know Amaya's insecure. Sometimes it's even painful to watch. But that's not an excuse for lying and acting hysterical and being two-faced. She asked me why we were icing her out and I told her. I mean, I'd been listening to Colin call her a tramp and Kaia call her a two-faced phony. Well, I'm not that type of guy. I'm a straight mover. I'll tell people how I feel. Really, though, it was Amaya who pushed the issue—not me. I told her how I felt about her. She could have used what I'd told her as an amazing learning tool, but from what I can tell it won't be taken as such. I told her she could have a clean slate, that I'd forgive but not forget.

She'll be walking through life far from a friend of mine. It's sad.

Kaia: I think the house left in a somewhat divided way. I couldn't map out the divisions, but I can say that no one's sure who anyone else is. I guess you could say I'm leaving on bad terms with Amaya. Initially, my engagement with her was limited. I think I was too strong and opinionated, and that was overbearing for her. But I think we had a mutual concern about how to communicate. So I went through a period of what you could call the beginning of a friendship with Amaya. *We're both intelligent human beings, both women, let's try,* I thought. But it didn't work out. When she saw who I was, what that actually meant, she ran away. She was quick to mistrust me. Until the last day, Amaya had never been up-front with me. And then, when she confronted me, it seemed really melodramatic and nonspecific. As far as I can tell, she just doesn't like that I'm a strong person. I was the last person she confronted, and ironically, in the end, I'm the only person she feels she mistrusts.

Teck: I think some of my roommates could be bullies, and that they bullied Amaya. But Amaya is so

sweet. Amaya is the most innocent cutest little girl you can imagine. She doesn't really hurt anybody. I think my roommates picked on her, because they knew they could. Amaya is too sweet for me to hit on. It's not a challenge. Someone who is weak is no challenge for me to try and make upset.

COLiN: During the last week in Hawaii, I felt sympathy for Amaya, but there's a point where making yourself comfortable, making yourself happy, outweighs all sympathy you will have for somebody else. I still completely realize what I saw in a person whom I really liked and I will cherish all the times we spent together that were wonderful, that were fun, that were beautiful.

But if I've learned anything else from being in Hawaii, it's if you have a problem with somebody, you need to go up to them. This process is about telling people how you feel, confronting people, and that's what I did. Was I motivated by Kaia and Matt? Well, it helped me to know how they felt, but regardless, at some point in time I would have told Amaya how I felt. I felt great after talking to her. When somebody is too negative and dragging your emotions down and not productively growing as a person, you remove that person from your life. As for Amaya and Tony, no, I did not care. It was amusing to me when I heard Amaya say, "We just clicked." I was thinking: *You click with anybody with a twig and berries.* As for Tony, he took seconds. Anytime you're pulling up the rear on the gravy train, you're in trouble.

JON MUrray, CreatOr: As with any situation, no one was completely right and no one was completely wrong. Hopefully everyone will learn something from watching the shows.

Matt KuNitZ, SupervisiNg PrODucer: The last week was sad to watch. I think most of the crew felt bad for Amaya. She is so vulnerable and her roommates were very hard on her. But the crew must remain objective and uninvolved. Times like those make our jobs difficult.

PaM: For me, Amaya was a breath of fresh air. She's fun and exciting and she was easy to get close to. I don't usually get close to someone so fast, but Amaya and I are really similar. I could see myself in her going through the things she was going through. I saw her as very normal compared to the rest of them. She's a sweetheart. She does everything with her heart, everything. She was very real. At the end of their time in Hawaii, I felt like she was used.

Everyone knew she was more sensitive and emotional. When Kaia, Matt and Colin confronted her and told her she wasn't "real," they broke her heart. She really felt sad and upset. I told her it was them and not her. Don't let what people you've known for only six months tell you who you are. It seemed unfair to me.

TECK: HONOLULU IS JUST TOO SMALL. PEOPLE WERE CONSTANTLY TELLING ME MY BUSINESS BEFORE IT WAS MY BUSINESS. EVERYWHERE I'D GO I'D GET A TECK REPORT.

THE ISLAND LIFE

KAIA: WHAT WILL I MISS MOST ABOUT HAWAII? THE WARMTH OF THE TEMPERATURE AND NOT HAVING ANYTHING TO DO. EVERYONE IN HAWAII WAS SO AFFECTIONATE. EVERYONE KISSED WHEN THEY SAW ONE ANOTHER.

Going Out

AMAYA: Going out at night in Waikiki was very Top 40. I had fun going out, but I heard a lot of ten-minute versions of "It Takes Two (to Make a Thing Go Right)."

World Cafe
500 Ala Moana Boulevard
Honolulu
The gang partied here on their second night. Ruthie partied a little too hard.

Bogart's Cafe and Espresso Bar
3045 Monsarrat Avenue
Honolulu
Right near the house, this is where Kaia and Matt would bond over grinds and coffee.

RUTHiE: Hawaii will always be home to me. I may end up living in New York, but I'll always think of Hawaii as a home. It represents my quiet side. And New York represents the wild side.

Eurasia
2552 Kalua Avenue
Honolulu

Club Rock-Za
1770 Kapiolani Boulevard
Honolulu
Ruthie and Teck got wild here lots of times.

Eggs'n Things
1911-B Kalakaua Avenue
Honolulu
Open all night! Where the cast would go after a hard night's clubbing.

Ocean's
Restaurant Row
500 Ala Moana Boulevard
Honolulu
The lapdance was here.

Mystique
Restaurant Row
Honolulu

Indigo
1121 Nu'uanu Avenue
Honolulu
Site of the Real World wrap party.

Moose McGillycuddy's Pub
310 Lewers Street
Waikiki Bazaar
Teck's wild birthday night was here.

Matt: My favorite Hawaiian sayings were "Gimme some aloha!" and "Show me your aloha!"

Don Ho's Paniolo Cafe
53-146 Kamehameha Highway
Honolulu
Where the group went for authentic native fare.

Duke's Canoe Club
Outrigger Waikiki Hotel
2335 Kalakaua Avenue
Honolulu
A group favorite.

TeCK: The most romantic spot in Hawaii was the beach down the street from our house. If you wanted, you could get your freak on.

HanoHano Room
Sheraton Waikiki Hotel
Honolulu
Amaya and Colin's first date was here!

Chili's
2350 Kuhio Avenue
Honolulu
Teck's favorite restaurant.

Real World-Hawaii's Favorite Beaches

Sandy's Beach
Tong's Beach
Maka Pu'u Tide Pools
Wimanalo Beach
Kilua Park Beach

Kirin Restaurant
2518 S. Beretania
Honolulu
Where Matt and Ruthie talked it out.

Nick's Fishmarket
2070 Kalakaua Avenue
Honolulu
One of Teck's favorite restaurants.

Sam Choy's Diamond Head Restaurant
449 Kapahulu Boulevard
Honolulu
Where Matt promised to take the roommates if they all did their chores.

COLiN: The thing I'll miss the most about Hawaii? The beach. I surfed practically every day.

Staying Home

COLIN: KAIA STOLE ALL OF AMAYA'S FOOD. SHE'D SPECIFICALLY NOT GO SHOPPING BECAUSE SHE THOUGHT THAT AMAYA HAD OVER-PURCHASED. SHE THOUGHT IF SHE DIDN'T HELP EAT THE FOOD, IT WOULD ALL GO TO WASTE.

Ruthie: The house was a mess. Our bathroom was skanky. It was a cute house, though. My favorite parts were my bed and the backyard. I liked the hot tub. I had sex in the hot tub twice, but I won't say any names. Let's just say there was a third person in the tub who was there on "camera watch" making sure nobody saw.

COLIN: Ruthie had sex in the hot tub and thought people weren't watching? There was a surveillance camera right there!

Amaya: The kitchen was a pigsty. And I can only describe the living room area as a weird, vast, tumbleweed garden. There would be these big lint balls everywhere. I don't know where they came from, but they were huge and disgusting. Oh, and the hickea had a scary stain on it. I can barely discuss it.

Teck: That hickea thing, whatever you call it, that was my second bed. Yeah, I had a few late-night guests there. And when we first got there, Kaia rubbed some oil on me when we were lying on it.

Matt: I clearly recall seeing Teck making love with a woman on the hickea. I walked in on him twice, actually.

Kaia: I was definitely one of the cleanest people in the house. I mean, Ruthie didn't ever do dishes; she didn't even know how to operate the dishwasher. And here's something viewers might not know about *The Real World*: you have to buy your own food. It's not like we had a lot of money. I was always getting blamed for stealing Amaya's food, but it was really Justin.

STOP taking any of my food. You did not pay for it, your name isn't on it! Please respect this! —Amaya

The Break-in

'Real World' gets a dose of anti-aloha

Star-Bulletin staff

MTV, welcome to the real world.

The television network's filming of its "Real World" series at a home in the here was interrupted by a burglary yesterday.

A 39-year-old Kalihi Valley man with a long criminal record was arrested for allegedly stealing a daily planner from the residence.

Footprints in the sand led East Honolulu Crime Reduction Unit officers to the suspect, who was taken into custody and booked for first-degree robbery at 4:15 a.m. yesterday. The burglary was reported at 3:25.

The suspect is one of three men convicted in 1982 for the 1980 murder of fellow prison inmate Milton Nihipali. His criminal record includes 28 prior arrests.

The man came in from the beach side of the property, on the Waikiki side of the Diamond Head lighthouse, and entered one of two houses where MTV is filming, police said.

He was observed by closed-circuit television cameras in the kitchen, where he allegedly took a daily planner. When confronted outside the residence by a crewmember, the suspect returned the item and fled.

Matt Kunitz, Supervising Producer: It was a Saturday night, about 3:30AM, and most cast members were asleep. Crew members were monitoring surveillance cameras, as they always do. Suddenly, they spotted a weird man wearing a sarong in the house. Next thing they know, he's stolen Matt's check book and day planner. Two of the guys from the crew caught him as he was running over the sea wall. It turned out he was a convicted murderer with a massive record. The house had news cameras parked outside. It was crazy. Within hours it was on CNN and even made the international news. The cast didn't even care, though.

Matt: That break-in came during the hell week when Ruthie was leaving the house. I hadn't slept at all. It was almost comedy that some lunatic had come and stolen my daily planner. But then it became a complete pain. I had to go to court at least three times.

THE FUTURE

Kaia: I'm going to explore acting, and I'm in the process of getting an acting coach. I'm writing my autobiography and I'd like to write some travel memoirs. I'd also like to explore independent filmmaking. Modeling, I'd do without a question. I'd like to do it for the photography itself. Anything that gives me the freedom to express my emotions....

Ruthie: The best perk from being on *The Real World* is the opportunity it presents. On the downside, we give up our lives, our stories, our dreams and fears. People are going to think the people we are now is who we'll be in two years—which is not true. This is not even the beginning for me. I want to do music video producing. I want to write.

I want to do lots of things. *The Real World* doesn't make you. You make you.

Teck: I'm going to go back to Atlanta to finish my movie, *Life's Suite.* I'm co-producing it and starring in it. Then it's off to California to finish my CD. Then, *The Real World-Road Rules Challenge.* I'll probably move to Los Angeles eventually, but I'll go wherever calls me.

Amaya: I'm pursuing a career in talent management and living in Southern California and trying to go about living my life day by day. I'm going on *The Challenge* to hopefully prove that I'm an intelligent person, not completely one-dimensional. I know it's going to be fun. I'm unemployed now, so I really want to win that prize money.

Colin: It's always changing. I went to summer school at Berkeley. Seven books in six weeks, which is pretty ridiculous. Otherwise, I've been meeting with lots of people, networks, and agencies. I'm thinking of transferring to UCLA, so I can be near the industry. I'm doing *The Challenge* in the fall, which technically means that for a semester I'm a college dropout. I really like saying that, I don't know why. Anyway, *The Challenge* should be interesting.

Amaya and I should be able to be civil. I hope.

Justin: I worked on Wall Street for the summer, and enjoyed being in the city—especially the East Village. After the show, I was hyper social, meeting people wherever I went. I'm going traveling for a while, and then I'll be going back to Harvard in the fall—with a whole different attitude and new hindsight.

Matt: I'm currently a production assistant on the show *NYPD Blue.* I'm working fifteen hours a day and learning to write and direct for television. I've been having some meetings and I'm making a lot of new friends and holding on to all of my true, pre-*Real World* friendships.

THE STATS

TECK'S *Favorites*

TV SHOW: *The Cosby Show, The A-Team*
BOOK: *The Seven Spiritual Laws of Success*
MOVIE: *Carwash*
CARTOON: *Fat Albert*
ACTOR: Lawrence Fishburne
ACTRESS: Amaya
COMEDIAN: Eddie Murphy
TOY: Transformers
FRUIT: Pineapple
VEGETABLE: Greens
DRINK: Cranberry juice
SANDWICH: A gondola
CAR: Ferrari
CD: Mary J. Blige, *My Life;* Michael Jackson *Off the Wall*
BAND: Jimi Hendrix Experience
AUTHOR: Matt
POET: Kaia
REAL WORLD: Hawaii and New York
ROAD RULES: Season One! With Carlos.
*REAL WORLD-*ER: Colin
*ROAD RULE-*R: Carlos
SPORT TO WATCH: Basketball
SPORT TO PLAY: Basketball, golf
WEB SITE: www.teck$$.com (doesn't yet exist!)
SCENT: Red Door/Jasmine (body oil)
HAIR COLOR: blonde
ITEM OF CLOTHING: Baggy cargo jeans and Woodruff high school football shirt
COLOR: Yellow and tan
MAGAZINE: *Vibe, Fortune* (because I will have one!)
MUSIC VIDEO: "Thriller," "Drop" by Pharcyde
VIDEO GAME: Mario Brothers
ACCESSORY: My silver bracelet from India
CLASS AT SCHOOL: Art class

AMAYA'S *Favorites*

TV SHOW: *The Golden Girls*
BOOK: *A Tree Grows in Brooklyn*
MOVIE: *The First Wives Club*
CARTOON: *South Park* and *Scooby Doo*
ACTOR: Harrison Ford
ACTRESS: Marilyn Monroe
COMEDIAN: Chris Rock
TOY: Mulan Makeover Magic Doll and the Laa-Laa Teletubbie
FRUIT: Peach
VEGETABLE: I hate vegetables!
DRINK: Lemonade
SANDWICH: French dip
CAR: Mine. Honda Prelude SI
CD: *Paul's Boutique, Graceland, Go soundtrack*
BAND: Beastie Boys
SINGER: Madonna
AUTHOR: Oscar Wilde
POET: Dorothy Parker
REAL WORLD: L.A. and San Francisco
ROAD RULES: Season Two
*REAL WORLD-*ER: Ruthie, Heather B., Neil
*ROAD RULE-*R: Timmy
SPORT TO WATCH: College basketball
SPORT TO PLAY: Ultimate Frisbee
WEB SITE: amazon.com
SCENT: Clinique Aromatic Elixir/Happy
HAIR COLOR: Red!
ITEM OF CLOTHING: Jeans
COLOR: Blue
MAGAZINE: *Marie Claire*
MUSIC VIDEO: "Bedtime Story" by Madonna
VIDEO GAME: Crash Bandicoot!
ACCESSORY: My watch! Wenger. I got it at Costco!
CLASS AT SCHOOL: Playwriting

MATT'S Favorites

TV SHOW: *NYPD Blue*
BOOK: *You Can't Be Neutral on a Moving Train*
CARTOON: *Terrance and Phillip*
ACTOR: Marlon Brando in *On the Waterfront*
ACTRESS: Claire Danes in *My So-Called Life*
COMEDIAN: Woody Allen
TOY: Irene's teddy dog
FRUIT: What is a fruitcake and why do people eat it?
VEGETABLE: Eggplant...except not!
DRINK: Most any adult beverage
SANDWICH: The one with two beautiful women and me in the middle. No mayo please!
CAR: My grandpa's taxi
CD: Ben Harper's *The Will to Live*
BAND: Dave Matthews Band
AUTHOR: Howard Zinn
POET: Alice Walker
REAL WORLD: Seattle
ROAD RULES: Semester at Sea
***REAL WORLD*-ER:** How cute is Lindsay!
***ROAD RULE*-R:** Yes. I hear he's nice.
SPORT TO WATCH: Football
SPORT TO PLAY: Football
WEB SITE: www.teck$$.com (Stay tuned!)
SCENT: Coffee in the morning
HAIR COLOR: Whatever Rodman's sporting.
ITEM OF CLOTHING: Blue tinted glasses
COLOR: Blue
MAGAZINE: Whichever one has Colin on the cover
MUSIC VIDEO: LL Cool J: "Mama Says Knock You Out"
VIDEO GAME: Ms. Pac-Man
ACCESSORY: Amaya's watch
CLASS AT SCHOOL: Advanced Screenwriting

KAIA'S Favorites

TV SHOW: Dramas like *Homicide*
BOOK: *Beloved*
MOVIE: None!
CARTOON: *Aeon Flux*
ACTOR: Allen Iverson
ACTRESS: Angela Bassett
COMEDIAN: Teck $$
FRUIT: Mango
VEGETABLE: Rutabaga
DRINK: Blue Hawaiian or Martini
SANDWICH: Two of me with a certain crew member in the middle
CAR: Old Jaguars
CD: *Kaya* by Bob Marley
BAND: None
AUTHOR: I have a lot!
POET: Langston Hughes
REAL WORLD: Haven't seen enough
ROAD RULES: Never saw it
***REAL WORLD*-ER:** Don't know
***ROAD RULE*-R:** Didn't watch
SPORT TO WATCH: Basketball
SPORT TO PLAY: Running
WEB SITE: random artistic sites
SCENT: Teck's underarm odor
HAIR COLOR: Natural
ITEM OF CLOTHING: None
COLOR: Every color
MAGAZINE: *The New Yorker*
MUSIC VIDEO: "Beat It" by Michael Jackson
VIDEO GAME: Uh, no.
ACCESSORY: My notebook
CLASS AT SCHOOL: Performance Art Class with Writing

COLIN'S *Favorites*

TV SHOW: *SportsCenter* and *The Late Show with Craig Kilborn*
BOOK: *The Big Show*
MOVIE: *Fast Times at Ridgemont High*
CARTOON: *Speedy Gonzales*
ACTOR: Sean Penn and Teck
ACTRESS: Amaya
COMEDIAN: Craig Kilborn
TOY: G.I. Joe
FRUIT: Mango
VEGETABLE: Corn on the cob
DRINK: Dr Pepper
SANDWICH: A Jennifer Lopez and Elisabeth Shue sandwich
CAR: 1979 VW Golf (must be missing right rear hubcap)
CD: *Kanetic Source featuring Teck $$*
BAND: NKOTB and Milli Vanilli
AUTHOR: Matt
POET: None
REAL WORLD: Seattle
ROAD RULES: Season Two
REAL WORLD-ER: Teck
ROAD RULE-R: Kalle
SPORT TO WATCH: Basketball
SPORT TO PLAY: Basketball
WEB SITE: www.espn.com
SCENT: DNA (discontinued and I was pissed!)
HAIR COLOR: Brunette
ITEM OF CLOTHING: G-string
COLOR: Blue
MAGAZINE: Honcho
MUSIC VIDEO: "Rico Suave" by Gerardo
VIDEO GAME: Pac-Man
ACCESSORY: Condoms
CLASS AT SCHOOL: African American Studies

RUTHIE'S *Favorites*

TV SHOW: *Sex and the City*
BOOK: The one I write.
MOVIE: *Beaches*
CARTOON: *South Park*
ACTOR: Eric Cartman
ACTRESS: Marilyn Monroe
COMEDIAN: Chris Rock
TOY: Jet-skis
FRUIT: Mango
VEGETABLE: Mushrooms-sautéed
DRINK: Hawaiian Sun Passion Orange
SANDWICH: Quarter Pounder
CAR: Porsche 911
CD: Go soundtrack
SINGER: Madonna
REAL WORLD: New York
ROAD RULES: None
REAL WORLD-ER: Pedro
ROAD RULE-R: Christina from *Road Rules—Australia*
SPORT TO WATCH: Basketball
SPORT TO PLAY: Wake Boarding
WEB SITE: None
SCENT: Plumeria
HAIR COLOR: Blonde
ITEM OF CLOTHING: My black g-string
COLOR: Red
MAGAZINE: *People*
MUSIC VIDEO: "Ironic" by Alanis Morrisette
VIDEO GAME: Any race car games
ACCESSORY: My nose ring, I feel naked without it.
CLASS AT SCHOOL: Women's Studies

THE CASTING

Casting The Real World

JASON: It's been a long road since I was on *The Real World*. After the show, I chilled in Arkansas, and then went to San Francisco to surf. Basically, I was doing nothing. Somehow, I managed to find a place to live for real cheap. Out of nowhere, Bunim/Murray Productions called me and asked me if I wanted to work for them for a while, do some consulting for *Road Rules–Latin America*. I was supposed to help with casting. I like talking to people. A lot of other interviewers are intimidated if the girls are pretty or if they come on to you too strong. I was just kinda myself and talked to them. Plus, I'd been through it before. I knew how they felt. I knew they'd be nervous. I'd try to ease them into the process, make them comfortable. I knew where they were coming from.

Then came the *Real World/Road Rules Challenge*. I did that. Afterward, I still didn't know what I was going to do with my life. Thank God for Drew. He's the supervising casting director, actually the guy who cast me for *The Real World—Boston*. He called me up. "Wanna come and be an associate casting director?" Certainly, I was nervous making the transition from cast to crew, but it's not like going from the Jedi to the Dark Side. It's not like that at all.

I was going in as a cast member. More than anything, I had the cast members' feelings at heart. I was thinking I could tell the applicants the truth, tell them how difficult being on the show can be, what a mind f**k it can be. "Look past the MTV fame," I warned them. "I'm not trying to scare you, but doing this show is a lot harder than it looks." Of course, no one heard what I said. There wasn't one person who stepped aside and said this wasn't the right time. Why would they?

I loved interviewing potential cast members. And now I have experience under my belt. I then went to work for *Road Rules* as an associate story editor. Being story editor—now that's crazy. It blows my mind how much production knows about the cast members, how much they knew about me.

There are people I passed every day in the office who knew some of my deepest darkest secrets. I felt like I was an asset to the other writers, because I had been a cast member. No one really knows what it's like unless they've experienced it. I was the resident cast member.

As for what I'm doing next? I don't really know. I've been working full days for a year now. I know it sounds insane, but I'm still not sure if a full-time job is my destiny. I'm learning a lot, still maturing. I'm twenty-six now. I'm watching footage of the cast partying, and I'm in a little office with a little window on deadline. Times sure have changed....

JASON ON THE CAST

ON AMAYA

I did a follow with Amaya down at UCLA. I went and picked her up at her sorority and took her to Jerry's Deli. She was sexy, witty, pretty, and cool. I had no idea what would happen to her on the season. I couldn't have predicted a relationship with Colin or the clingy behavior I hear she's exhibited.

ON Matt

I thought Matt was real slick. He didn't really have a positive impact on me. Everybody else in casting loved him. They couldn't get enough of him. He was like the golden boy. I figured they were seeing something I didn't see.

ON COLiN

I didn't see that coming, but it made sense. He's very unassuming, a normal kid, straightforward, self-effacing in a funny way, secure, but young.

ON RUTHiE

Ruthie rocks. We got Ruthie's tape and application way late. It was total fate that she got on the show. We had already done all the casting, but there was still a vacant spot. Watching her tape, we were like,

"Check this out." She's beautiful. She's not a bougie white person. We did an interview with her over the phone, liked her, flew her in, and she went straight to finals. Come to think of it, it might have been the fastest casting ever. She was on the show in one week. For her follow, we went shopping with her at Red Balls on Melrose. She was completely unabashed, putting on feather boas, going wild. She was totally someone I would hang out with. She's not intimidated. I knew then and there that she'd fit right in.

ON Kaia

I didn't have a lot of interaction with Kaia. I sat in on her final interview. I had no idea why they chose her over this other girl, Jen, who incidentally was a friend of mine. I guess somebody up high really liked her. What can I say?

ON TeCK

I found his tape, put it in the VCR and instantly knew he'd be on the show. I laughed my ass off watching that tape. It was just Teck being Teck. *Road Rules* also wanted him. It was actually kind of a fight. But he's older, so he got on *The Real World*.

Excerpts from Teck's Casting Application

NAME: Tecumshea, Teck BIRTHDATE: January 26, 1976

SIBLINGS (NAMES AND AGES): Taqwana Daniella, 19

WHAT IS YOUR ETHNIC BACKGROUND? Black with a pinch or two of Native American (Indian)

EDUCATION: NAME OF HIGH SCHOOL AND YEAR COMPLETED: Woodruff High School, Peoria, Illinois, 4 years completed

NAME OF COLLEGE: Morris Brown College, 2 years completed. My major was Theater Arts, Radio, TV, and Film

OTHER EDUCATION: School of firsthand experience.

WHERE DO YOU WORK? DESCRIBE YOUR JOB HISTORY: I work at California Pizza Kitchen. I've worked all types of jobs: retail, restaurants, digging holes, unloading trucks, detassling corn, etc...

WHAT IS YOUR ULTIMATE CAREER GOAL? I want to own a multimedia production company and TV station like Ted Turner. I want to control the world like Ted.

WHAT ARTISTIC TALENTS DO YOU HAVE (MUSIC, ART, DANCE, PERFORMANCE, WRITING, ETC.) HOW SKILLED ARE YOU? I'm an MC. My roommate (Kanetic Source) raps and I'm his hype man. We're pretty damn good. I also dance. I enjoy acting, and I sometimes play drums.

HOW WOULD SOMEONE WHO REALLY KNOWS YOU DESCRIBE YOUR BEST TRAITS? It's my unpredictability. I keep people on their toes. It's almost never a dull moment with me. It's also my charm. I could probably charm Hillary Clinton into pleasuring me.

HOW WOULD SOMEONE WHO REALLY KNOWS YOU DESCRIBE YOUR WORST TRAITS? It's my unpredictability. I'm not easily read. Sometimes I'm Mr. Scatterbrain. It can sometimes get on people's nerves. Plus I'm loud.

TECK: I actually tried to get on *The Real World* the year before. I went to auditions in Atlanta. I wrote on my application, "Women are like potato chips, you can't eat just one." I think Leola, the casting person, got offended. So I didn't get on. My stars weren't in line with each other then.

DO YOU HAVE A BOYFRIEND OR GIRLFRIEND? I don't have a girlfriend, because they are too nagging. I am a very free spirit. I can't be tied down.

HOW IMPORTANT IS SEX TO YOU? DO YOU HAVE IT ONLY WHEN YOU'RE IN A RELATIONSHIP OR DO YOU SEEK IT OUT AT OTHER TIMES? HOW DID IT COME ABOUT ON THE LAST OCCASION? Sex is very important. I love to have sex. I can't just have sex with one person. It gets boring. I love women. That's my No. 1 problem. Too many women, not enough time or money. The mo' sex, the mo' better. I don't sleep with every girl that I date and some girls can't take "no" for an answer! I feel more guys should start saying no to some of these chicks. Maybe we'll be more appreciated.

DESCRIBE YOUR FANTASY DATE: Two women (Pamela Lee and Tracy Bingham). One beach house, a bearskin rug, a hot tub, and me.

OTHER THAN A BOYFRIEND OR GIRLFRIEND, WHO'S THE MOST IMPORTANT PERSON IN YOUR LIFE RIGHT NOW? Probably my sister. She goes to Xavier University in New Orleans. I worry about her safety and I just want her to have the best in life.

IF YOU HAD TO DESCRIBE YOUR MOTHER BY DIVIDING HER PERSONALITY INTO TWO PARTS, HOW WOULD YOU DESCRIBE EACH PART? My mother is so beautiful. She is the ideal woman. Caring, respectful, humble. She can cook, sew, help you with your homework, and give you a word of advice. She can also be nagging, too passive, and sometimes bitchy. But I love my momma!

IF YOU HAD TO DESCRIBE YOUR FATHER BY DIVIDING HIS PERSONALITY INTO TWO PARTS, HOW WOULD YOU DESCRIBE EACH PART? My dad is the bomb. He gave me my personality. My father is a minister, so he's a great orator. He's very smooth. He's the Casanova type. He's handsome, intelligent, smart, and a charmer. But he's also a Scorpio. If you cross him, he can be very cold and vindictive. I love my pops, too.

WHAT ARE YOUR THOUGHTS ON SEXUAL ORIENTATIONS? I'm not gay! And I never will be. But I do enjoy the company of a couple of sexy lesbians.

IF YOU HAD ALADDIN'S LAMP AND THREE WISHES, WHAT WOULD THEY BE? I would wish that my parents never got divorced. I would wish that everyone was one color (black). And then I would wish for an $80 million NBA contract with the Lakers. I like Shaq and Kobe's game.

True Casting Confession:

Why I Should Be on The Real World.

TECK: So far, the brothers who've been on the show, there have been no leaders. I'm a leader. I'm not a follower. If everyone is going south, I'm going to go northeast. I can take a situation that happened in the house and relate it to the young, especially the brothers and sisters. That's who I really want to touch since I will be the token black person in the house. I don't have to do what America wants me to do. I don't have to listen to hip-hop. I can put on some Shania Twain or listen to Fiona Apple all day. I don't have to put on Janet Jackson or Mariah Carey just because America thinks it's what I should do. I'm a leader.

So I want to show that, definitely. I'm a trailblazer. You know, it could be a big rainforest out there and by the time I'm done with it, it's cut down.

Excerpts from Ruthie's Casting Application

NAME: Ruthie **BIRTHDATE:** Sepember 14, 1977

SIBLINGS (NAMES AND AGES): Sara, 21; Silverius, 21; Rachel, 22

WHAT IS YOUR ETHNIC BACKGROUND? Samoan/Filipino/Spanish/Irish/French

EDUCATION: NAME OF HIGH SCHOOL AND YEAR COMPLETED: James Campbell High School, Class of '95 (four years)

NAME OF COLLEGE: Rutgers University, New Brunswick, New Jersey, Journalism and Mass Media, Class of 2000. Three years completed!

OTHER EDUCATION: University of Manoa, 1995-96

WHERE DO YOU WORK? DESCRIBE YOUR JOB HISTORY. Right now I tutor eight students in exposition writing.

WHAT IS YOUR ULTIMATE CAREER GOAL? I have many! I'd like to start my own magazine. And ultimately I want to express my creative talents as a music video producer. I just hope Madonna's still around when I become a "professional." I definitely want to work on a song with her!

WHAT ARTISTIC TALENTS DO YOU HAVE (MUSIC, ART, DANCE, PERFORMANCE, WRITING, ETC.) HOW SKILLED ARE YOU? I write a lot of poetry and love going to open-mike sessions to read them. I also do rap performances.

HOW WOULD SOMEONE WHO REALLY KNOWS YOU DESCRIBE YOUR BEST TRAITS? I think the most common trait I've heard is genuine. My friends who know me best say I've got a lot of heart and I sincerely care about people, even strangers! My friends say I can be too friendly, but hey, it's the Aloha spirit.

HOW WOULD SOMEONE WHO REALLY KNOWS YOU DESCRIBE YOUR WORST TRAITS? I repeat myself. I can never remember who I've told what story to—maybe it's because I speak to too many people.

I'm charmingly blunt, sometimes too blunt. I'll say whatever comes to my mind. My friends say Ruthie does whatever she wants because she can. (They're right about that!)

RUTHIE: It was a gut feeling that made me apply for *The Real World.* People kept coming up to me and randomly telling me I could make it on the show. I was like, "Why is everyone telling me this?" I thought it was a sign. But it was too late. It was already November, and as I understood it, casting was over. I was sitting in Shakespeare class, and I just couldn't stop thinking about *The Real World.* The second I got out of class, I ran to the computer lab, got onto the Web. My suspicions were confirmed: casting calls were over. There was an e-mail address, though. I sent a note, completely lying. It went something like this: "Dear Casting, This is urgent. I sent my video but I don't think you saw it." Then I described who I was and why I needed to be on the show. The next thing I knew I was making a video. Then I'm flying to Los Angeles for the finals. When I was at the Bunim/Murray offices, I ran into Gladys from *Road Rules*. She was hanging out there. She was incredibly discouraging. She told me, "Don't get your hopes up."

That one e-mail changed my life.

True Casting Confession:
Why I Should Be on The Real World.

I know there's a lot that goes on behind the scenes. I know there's a lot of things that people on the show go through. I know they learned a lot about other people and about themselves. I know some people didn't work out. But still, I think it's a really great experience. And, no, I don't think it's gonna be a five-month party. If I make it, which I hope I do, I won't hold back. It's like, you ask me something, and I'll say it. That's it.

DO YOU HAVE A BOYFRIEND OR GIRLFRIEND? Yes, I have a beautiful girlfriend. I've never been committed to anyone in any of my previous relationships because I'm just too wild to settle down with ONE person. But there's something about Jess that changed my mind. She calls me at least once a day. We talk for hours. I love her voice! She's awesome to me. I absolutely adore Jess. The funny thing is she's the opposite of me, quiet. Maybe she balances me!

HOW IMPORTANT IS SEX TO YOU? It's funny you asked. Sex is very important to me. I love it. Throughout most of our relationship, Jess didn't care that I slept around. But *now,* I made a decision that I'm not sharing my body with anyone but Jess. This monogamous thing is new to me, but I kind of like it. Geez! You want to know about my last sexual episode? Okay. It was at a hotel in Hawaii with Jess—right after cheesecake, candlelight, and wine! (I told you she was romantic!)

DESCRIBE YOUR FANTASY DATE: Being flown by helicopter to an awaiting yacht in the middle of the Pacific Ocean at sunset. A room full of candles awaits me. In the middle of the floor, dinner is set on a Japanese-style table with plush pillows for seats. Dinner must be a gourmet *chicken* dinner. I love chicken!

WHO'S THE MOST IMPORTANT PERSON IN YOUR LIFE RIGHT NOW? I would say my two sisters, especially my older sister, Rachel. She loves me unconditionally and no matter what she's going though, she never takes it out on me. She listens to me, accepts me, and I just want to make her proud. She'll sacrifice a meal so I can eat.

IF YOU HAD TO DESCRIBE YOUR MOTHER BY DIVIDING HER PERSONALITY INTO TWO PARTS, HOW WOULD YOU DESCRIBE EACH PART? I didn't grow up with my mom, but I'll describe my foster parent Isabel, who I called Grandma. One part hugged me and said "I love you." But the other part told me I wasn't worth much and I'd grow up to be like my mom, whose footsteps I am *not* following. She believed in me, but she was old-fashioned in her thinking and didn't trust the outside world. She was always paranoid I was up to something.

IF YOU HAD TO DESCRIBE YOUR FATHER BY DIVIDING HIS PERSONALITY INTO TWO PARTS, HOW WOULD YOU DESCRIBE EACH PART? I didn't grow up with my dad, either, so I'll describe my foster father, Benjamin, who I called Grandpa. I couldn't get too close to my grandfather. One part of him was mean and harsh, then the next part reminisced about the good old days. I just stay around for the stories. I learned a lot.

WHAT ARE YOUR THOUGHTS ON SEXUAL ORIENTATIONS? Whatever floats your boat is fine with me.

CASTING MATT

Excerpts from Matt's Casting Application

NAME: Matt BIRTHDATE: December 22, 1976

SIBLINGS (NAMES AND AGES): Jonathan, 20

WHAT IS YOUR ETHNIC BACKGROUND? I'm pretty fly for a white guy!

EDUCATION: NAME OF HIGH SCHOOL AND YEAR COMPLETED: Torrey Pines High School in Del Mar, California. I graduated in 1995 with honors. (Who didn't at that snotty little rich school?)

NAME OF COLLEGE: UCLA, in my third year.

OTHER EDUCATION: Numerous classes in screenwriting and TV writing.

WHERE DO YOU WORK? DESCRIBE YOUR JOB HISTORY. My primary job is a part-time gig as a talk-show host on AM 1150, a sports/entertainment talk-radio station in Los Angeles. I've been working since I was fourteen years old. At first I was a busboy, then a waiter, then I got my first job in radio.

WHAT IS YOUR ULTIMATE CAREER GOAL? I want to be an English teacher and a writer. I'm going to be an extraordinary writer someday. I already am. I have written one screenplay. And I have an idea for a television show. As you can tell, I'm a dreamer. But I'm a dreamer with a message.

WHAT ARTISTIC TALENTS DO YOU HAVE (MUSIC, ART, DANCE, PERFORMANCE, WRITING, ETC.) HOW SKILLED ARE YOU? Writing. I pen poetry.

HOW WOULD SOMEONE WHO REALLY KNOWS YOU DESCRIBE YOUR BEST TRAITS? My best friends and family would tell you I'm complex, deep, intriguing, amazing, and kind. (Okay, so I'm a total stranger to modesty.) Seriously, those who know me understand my intelligence and insight into how the world works and how people work. They would tell you my intelligence is contagious. My complexity makes me intriguing. The people who really know me have witnessed my kindness and generosity. I have the ability to place myself in another person's shoes or world. I'm always there to listen to a friend in need. I have advice for everyone. And, finally, those who really know me would tell you I'm amazing (most likely), because I'm ambitious and they believe in me.

Matt: I went to an open call at the Magic Johnson Theaters in Los Angeles. I had no idea what percentage of people would be called back. I had fun with interviews. I didn't think I'd make it. I thought that would be the end of the road. But then I got into the semifinals. I kept telling myself it wasn't a big deal whether I made it or not. I had school and a job lined up, I had a real life ahead of me. But then, at some point between the semis and finals, I thought, *No, I do care. I want this. I want people to know and see me.*

HOW WOULD SOMEONE WHO REALLY KNOWS YOU DESCRIBE YOUR WORST TRAITS? Some people would argue I'm overly opinionated. A close friend of mine recently told me that I never shut up and listen. She said I'm too quick to give advice. I guess this is a character flaw of mine. Rather than listen and keep quiet, I prefer to tell people what they should do to correct their problems, to right their ship, if you will. I'm an "advice giver" through and through.

DESCRIBE YOUR MOST EMBARRASSING MOMENT IN LIFE: I lied to a twenty-three-year-old girl and told her I was twenty when I was really nineteen. We went to a club and I got carded by the bouncer—I think his name was Biff. It was humiliating.

DO YOU HAVE A BOYFRIEND OR GIRLFRIEND? I am currently single.

DESCRIBE YOUR FANTASY DATE: My house. I'm cooking. Marsala marinara with chicken over penne. Salad. Bread. Red wine. Jazz music. The table is beautiful. My date is beautiful. Next we go dancing. At a casual place. Lots of slow songs. We bond. We fall in love. Then we go to the beach with a blanket and a bottle of wine...

OTHER THAN A BOYFRIEND OR GIRLFRIEND, WHO'S THE MOST IMPORTANT PERSON IN YOUR LIFE RIGHT NOW? A toss-up. Either my brother or my partner at the radio station.

IF YOU HAD TO DESCRIBE YOUR MOTHER BY DIVIDING HER PERSONALITY INTO TWO PARTS, HOW WOULD YOU DESCRIBE EACH PART? Part One: workaholic. My mother's a tireless worker. She has a B.A., a Master's, and a Ph.D., which she earned in about thirteen months. Part Two: Worried sick.

IF YOU HAD TO DESCRIBE YOUR FATHER BY DIVIDING HIS PERSONALITY INTO TWO PARTS, HOW WOULD YOU DESCRIBE EACH PART? Part One: the geeky introvert. My dad's an unemotional guy. He can be withdrawn and volatile. Part Two: The teenage socialite. Ironically, my father also likes to schmooze. He can talk strangers' ears off. He can be really outgoing, especially concerning his pride regarding his sons.

WHAT ARE YOUR THOUGHTS ON SEXUAL ORIENTATIONS? I love gay people.

IF YOU HAD ALADDIN'S LAMP AND THREE WISHES, WHAT WOULD THEY BE? 1. Eternal happiness—meaning professional satisfaction and familial bliss. 2. An end to violence. 3. No child abuse.

True Casting Confession:
Why I Should Be on The Real World.

Matt: If you get me alone in a house with peers, friends, roommates, the walls will come down. And it will be pretty interesting. You'll see uproarious laughter and you'll see tears, and you'll see anger. You know, nothing violent, but I'm an outspoken guy with a lot of inner emotion. I think that I'd be right for a show like this. I could see myself doing this every day for five months, looking at my friend the camera. I think it's kind of fun.

EXcerpts from Amaya's Casting Application

NAME: Amaya BIRTHDATE: September 17, 1977

SIBLINGS (NAMES AND AGES): Diana (half-sister), 28; Lara, 17

WHAT IS YOUR ETHNIC BACKGROUND? Spanish American/Basque and Jewish

EDUCATION: NAME OF HIGH SCHOOL AND YEAR COMPLETED: Bishop O'Dowd High School, four years completed

NAME OF COLLEGE: UCLA. Just graduated.

WHERE DO YOU WORK? DESCRIBE YOUR JOB HISTORY. I guess right now I'm a freelance baby-sitter.

WHAT IS YOUR ULTIMATE CAREER GOAL? I would eventually like to be a film producer. First, however, I would like to be a talent agent. Then a talent manager and then end up a producer after I've established myself and made enough contacts.

WHAT ARTISTIC TALENTS DO YOU HAVE (MUSIC, ART, DANCE, PERFORMANCE, WRITING, ETC.) HOW SKILLED ARE YOU? I can sing, draw, and sculpt.

HOW WOULD SOMEONE WHO REALLY KNOWS YOU DESCRIBE YOUR BEST TRAITS? My best friends say I'm loyal. I try to be as true a friend as I can be. I'm kind of a mom, albeit a goofy mom among my friends. I like to think I have a good sense of humor. I tend to see the lighter side of things. I'm compassionate, I think. I just love people and can get very affectionate.

HOW WOULD SOMEONE WHO REALLY KNOWS YOU DESCRIBE YOUR WORST TRAITS? I'm very self-critical and can put myself down sometimes. This is often hard on relationships I have. I would love to love myself a little bit more, but I don't know how to. I want to learn to build my self-esteem. Lack thereof is my greatest flaw.

DESCRIBE YOUR MOST EMBARRASSING MOMENT IN LIFE: I went to Price Club with my mom and her friend on the first day of my period, insisting my cramps would not bother me. Well, when we got there, I walked to the furniture section and basically passed out in a La-Z-Boy. My cramps were so bad I couldn't walk, so my mom put me in the shopping cart and wheeled me around as she shopped.

Amaya: I went to an open casting call with my best friend. Actually, we both got interviewed. It was totally a lark, and initially I went out for *Road Rules*. I really dug the idea of *Semester at Sea*.

Why I Should Be on The Real World.

AMaya: I want just the hardest situation that there could possibly be so that later on in life things are going to be a piece of cake. I don't believe in boredom, I just believe that there's uninteresting people, so I would never be bored. I'm being as honest as I possibly can here. Really, I think I need to be knocked down a peg or two. I need somebody to discipline me, not in a sexual way, but I think someone needs to challenge me, something needs to challenge me. I would love just to show the world how to be a little more open-minded, a little more kind and a little more accepting. And that's all I want to be—just a firecracker out there. Get ready, I want to be there.

DO YOU HAVE A BOYFRIEND OR GIRLFRIEND? No boyfriend! After the last couple of guys, I think I need a little break.

HOW IMPORTANT IS SEX TO YOU? DO YOU HAVE IT ONLY WHEN YOU'RE IN A RELATIONSHIP OR DO YOU SEEK IT OUT AT OTHER TIMES? HOW DID IT COME ABOUT ON THE LAST OCCASION? My old philosophy was I only had sex with boyfriends. This summer, that changed and I foolishly slept around. I'm honestly a bit ashamed of myself. Ten partners in five years almost seems too much to me. Now, it seems like sex just fills a void. I don't feel as alone. I need someone to care about.

DESCRIBE YOUR FANTASY DATE: An incredibly charming, funny, decent-looking guy who can dance, takes me out for a wonderful dinner (Japanese food!), then dancing, then to the beach, builds me a fire and we sit there laughing and talking until the sun comes up.

OTHER THAN A BOYFRIEND OR GIRLFRIEND, WHO'S THE MOST IMPORTANT PERSON IN YOUR LIFE RIGHT NOW? My best friend Justin, whom I've known since I was thirteen. We are so much alike. Our senses of humor meld nicely.

IF YOU HAD TO DESCRIBE YOUR MOTHER BY DIVIDING HER PERSONALITY INTO TWO PARTS, HOW WOULD YOU DESCRIBE EACH PART? My mother is a guiding light and a friend. She has led me from infancy to adulthood, nurturing and guiding me along the way. She is a warm and wonderful human being. Over the years, my mother has also become a friend I can laugh with and go to for advice.

IF YOU HAD TO DESCRIBE YOUR FATHER BY DIVIDING HIS PERSONALITY INTO TWO PARTS, HOW WOULD YOU DESCRIBE EACH PART? My father is my teacher and my foil. He has taught me a lot about life and the world we live in, as well as teaching me a lot about humanity. He is my foil because we are so much alike, we almost cancel each other out. Some of my greatest schemes have been foiled by him.

WHAT ARE YOUR THOUGHTS ON SEXUAL ORIENTATIONS? I'm very accepting of homosexual lifestyles.

IF YOU HAD ALADDIN'S LAMP AND THREE WISHES, WHAT WOULD THEY BE? First, that this world could live in peace and satisfaction for the rest of eternity. Secondly, I would wish for a bountifully healthy environment with self-renewing resources (Thanks, Dad! I'm a tree hugger!). Lastly, I would wish for my family, my friends, and myself to live out the rest of our lives healthfully and happily and to be stinking rich and each own our own tropical islands with mini airstrips for our private planes.

CASTING COLIN

EXCERPTS FROM COLIN'S CASTING APPLICATION

NAME: Colin BIRTHDATE: November 8, 1979

SIBLINGS (NAMES AND AGES): Ryan, 22

WHAT IS YOUR ETHNIC BACKGROUND? Spanish, Puerto Rican, German, Danish

EDUCATION: NAME OF HIGH SCHOOL AND YEAR COMPLETED: Westlake High School, four years.

NAME OF COLLEGE: UC Berkeley, two semesters.

WHERE DO YOU WORK? DESCRIBE YOUR JOB HISTORY. I've worked at Macaroni Grill and Round Table Pizza.

WHAT IS YOUR ULTIMATE CAREER GOAL? Sports broadcasting, whether it be play-by-play announcing or doing sports for a news station (TV or radio). I would also like to start acting in school and maybe pursue that on the side.

COLIN: Beggars can't be choosers, so when I went to that open call I would have been happy to do *Road Rules* or *Real World*. I saw the ad for the open call in the newspaper. Trevor stayed back to go to class, but then he showed up at the last moment. We actually went to Mary-Ellis' table. Mary-Ellis said to Trevor, "Why don't you ask Sol something that will embarrass her?" He asked an obscene question, which she gave a really good answer to. You only get a certain time at the table. Mary-Ellis stopped us and told us we had a really interesting dynamic. So, we went out back and this guy Glenn started asking us questions. We started f**king around with him. We thought maybe we'd get a second on the casting special as rejects. They told us if we don't get calls by Sunday, we wouldn't get in it. Of course, they didn't call. Two weeks later, they let us know we were going to be on the casting special.

COLIN, MIKE AND TREVOR

HOW WOULD SOMEONE WHO REALLY KNOWS YOU DESCRIBE YOUR BEST TRAITS? I can be extremely charming and really fun to be around. My sense of humor is definitely one of my best traits. I'm very loyal to those that I care about as friends. The people who get close to me are those I will do anything for.

HOW WOULD SOMEONE WHO REALLY KNOWS YOU DESCRIBE YOUR WORST TRAITS? I am very stubborn when it comes to many things. My personality, especially my sarcasm, can be overbearing. Many times I rub people the wrong way. I get annoyed easily and I annoy others easily.

DESCRIBE YOUR MOST EMBARRASSING MOMENT IN LIFE: Falling in this school rally and taking a picture of my penis with some random camera when I was drunk and having the picture get around to all my friends.

DO YOU HAVE A BOYFRIEND OR GIRLFRIEND? I wish I had a girlfriend.

HOW IMPORTANT IS SEX TO YOU? DO YOU HAVE IT ONLY WHEN YOU'RE IN A RELATIONSHIP OR DO YOU SEEK IT OUT AT OTHER TIMES? HOW DID IT COME ABOUT ON THE LAST OCCASION? I haven't had sex outside a relationship, but I am definitely not against that. Hormones pretty much dominate how I think.

DESCRIBE YOUR FANTASY DATE: Candlelight dinner on a small tropical island with just me and my date. A live jazz band would be there and we would spend the night on blankets on the sand near the water.

OTHER THAN A BOYFRIEND OR GIRLFRIEND, WHO'S THE MOST IMPORTANT PERSON IN YOUR LIFE RIGHT NOW? I can't distinguish between my mom, dad, brother, and Trevor. They all care for me and I for them and that is why they are important. Because they are there for me whenever.

IF YOU HAD TO DESCRIBE YOUR MOTHER BY DIVIDING HER PERSONALITY INTO TWO PARTS, HOW WOULD YOU DESCRIBE EACH PART? Caring and loving/intelligent and socially wise.

IF YOU HAD TO DESCRIBE YOUR FATHER BY DIVIDING HIS PERSONALITY INTO TWO PARTS, HOW WOULD YOU DESCRIBE EACH PART? Loving/cares for family

WHAT ARE YOUR THOUGHTS ON SEXUAL ORIENTATIONS? I don't know exactly what this question is asking...but I like sex!

IF YOU HAD ALADDIN'S LAMP AND THREE WISHES, WHAT WOULD THEY BE? To find the woman of my dreams. To get hired by a sportscaster or another TV show. Lastly, that you want me to go to Hawaii.

True Casting Confession:

Why I Should Be on The Real World.

COLiN: Doing all the follows for the casting special has been awesome. I've met people who you wouldn't necessarily have met but you just click with. Whether or not they get picked, I'm glad I met those people. It's an awesome experience meeting people from totally different areas of society. I can see a little bit what it's like for people to live in a *Real World* house. You're thrown in with these people and you learn where they're coming from and I think it definitely helps people grow. Thrown into that situation, your whole mind-set gets shaken up. I seriously think that this is probably one of the best times if not the best time of my life. I've gotten so much out of this casting process. I can't even imagine what doing the show would be like.

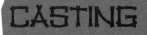
Excerpts from Kaia's Casting Application

NAME: Kaia née Margaret **BIRTHDATE:** August 24, 1976

SIBLINGS (NAMES AND AGES): None

WHAT IS YOUR ETHNIC BACKGROUND? Jewish/Eastern European Gypsy

EDUCATION: NAME OF HIGH SCHOOL AND YEAR COMPLETED: University of Chicago Laboratory School, Chicago, Illinois

NAME OF COLLEGE: UC Berkeley, seven semesters

OTHER EDUCATION: University of Iowa, two years; University of Dar-es-Salaam, Tanzania

WHERE DO YOU WORK? DESCRIBE YOUR JOB HISTORY. I've had so many wait-ressing jobs, I can't count them...I recently taught elementary school—first-graders. Now I model, dance, whatever brings the money! Oh, and freelance writing.

WHAT IS YOUR ULTIMATE CAREER GOAL? Writing while traveling around, and international law. Also, I will be in movies!

HOW WOULD SOMEONE WHO REALLY KNOWS YOU DESCRIBE YOUR BEST TRAITS? He/she would say that I'm fun, spontaneous, energetic, exciting, mysterious. I always add something noticeable to an environment. They would say that I'm direct and say what I mean.

HOW WOULD SOMEONE WHO REALLY KNOWS YOU DESCRIBE YOUR WORST TRAITS? I can be cold. Unknowingly. I think I'm being honest, but I can scare people with my lioness qualities. Sometimes people say I attract too much attention. And I expect too much from people while I'm the center of it all. I've been told my best traits are also my worst traits. I take everything to the extreme.

DESCRIBE YOUR MOST EMBARRASSING MOMENT IN LIFE: Getting an e-mail from the wife of a professor who found a letter he had intended to send to me, which described the various ways he would like to make me orgasm. She listed them. Imagine my surprise when she showed up in class. Oh, and told many people in the depart-ment...evidence in hand! That s**t was sick!

Kaia: The whole casting process felt like a big test. I felt like they were testing me on whether I was really confident, whether I could truly reveal myself. I actually really enjoyed it. People I didn't know were coming at me, challenging me about things I'd said in previous interviews, on my application. It was all about testing character strength.

DO YOU HAVE A BOYFRIEND OR GIRLFRIEND? Nope. I dabble here and there. First, everything must be tight as hell physically and immediately after, I must be wooed with intellect. I like being watched doing things: bathing, sleeping, masturbating. For me, if a man doesn't look at me, really see me, especially during sex, it's over.

HOW IMPORTANT IS SEX TO YOU? DO YOU HAVE IT ONLY WHEN YOU'RE IN A RELATIONSHIP OR DO YOU SEEK IT OUT AT OTHER TIMES? HOW DID IT COME ABOUT ON THE LAST OCCASION? Sex is plentiful when I want it to be. I seek it a lot but I'm careful nowadays 'cuz people are psycho. Sexual relationships to me are very necessary even if it is just people who turn you on in the places you go. You could say I invoke sexual desire a lot!

DESCRIBE YOUR FANTASY DATE: Skydiving and plunging into cold-ass water, swimming to shore, drinking some tropical stuff, making love...eating fruit, squeezing the juice on my body and demanding it be licked off.

OTHER THAN A BOYFRIEND OR GIRLFRIEND, WHO'S THE MOST IMPORTANT PERSON IN YOUR LIFE RIGHT NOW? Me. I have a lot to do for the next sixty-five to eighty-five years. This is the foundation and it's all up to me to make it work!!

IF YOU HAD TO DESCRIBE YOUR MOTHER BY DIVIDING HER PERSONALITY INTO TWO PARTS, HOW WOULD YOU DESCRIBE EACH PART? Adventurous and experimental while down-to-earth and easy to talk to.

IF YOU HAD TO DESCRIBE YOUR FATHER BY DIVIDING HIS PERSONALITY INTO TWO PARTS, HOW WOULD YOU DESCRIBE EACH PART? Very self-confident/arrogant, patient and creative.

WHAT ARE YOUR THOUGHTS ON SEXUAL ORIENTATIONS? Not a problem with me.

IF YOU HAD ALADDIN'S LAMP AND THREE WISHES, WHAT WOULD THEY BE? Everything I accomplish makes me famous while I am alive. To give my mother a life of excitement (travel). To help restructure politics so that those on the bottom can see justice.

True Casting Confession:

Why I Should Be on The Real World.

Kaia: If I get on the show, this would be the first time in my life that I'm actually allowing people to see who I am. That would put me in a vulnerable position—where I've never been before. I feel like that's one of those things I want to conquer a little bit. I think it's really interesting that there are some people who get on the show and get really pissed off and upset because their privacy is being intruded upon. Yeah, people don't realize how intense it is. But that's what the public is interested in: the intimate moments. I think I'm ready to show some of mine, to be one of the real people doing real things having a real good time.

EXCERPTS FROM JUSTIN'S CASTING APPLICATION

NAME: Justin **BIRTHDATE:** September 16, 1977

SIBLINGS (NAMES AND AGES): Christopher, 19

WHAT IS YOUR ETHNIC BACKGROUND? I'm a white boy. Dad is mega–Aryan Scandinavianesque. And Mom is white with pretty black hair.

EDUCATION: NAME OF HIGH SCHOOL AND YEAR COMPLETED: Kingwood High School. I suffered through two years before fleeing.

NAME OF COLLEGE: Simon's Rock College, two years. Swarthmore College, two years.

OTHER EDUCATION: Language Institute (Hebrew/Arabic), Hebrew University, Jerusalem

WHERE DO YOU WORK? DESCRIBE YOUR JOB HISTORY. I'm now a teaching fellow at Harvard College. Back in Philadelphia, I worked at a youth shelter doing outreach, needle exchange, transgender work.

WHAT IS YOUR ULTIMATE CAREER GOAL? It's arrogant to say I've settled on one by this point. I'll list some savory options: Gay/Lesbian civil rights attorney; academic professor writing lots of scary books; novelist; transgender activist.

WHAT ARTISTIC TALENTS DO YOU HAVE (MUSIC, ART, DANCE, PERFORMANCE, WRITING, ETC.) HOW SKILLED ARE YOU? Call me Liberace without the ruffles. Played the piano since I was in diapers. When I was transferring colleges, I almost went to Juilliard or the Oberlin Conservatory. But oh, life choices.

HOW WOULD SOMEONE WHO REALLY KNOWS YOU DESCRIBE YOUR BEST TRAITS? I think it would be a combination of two things. First, my intelligence. Just being able to absorb and wrap my mind around things, test assumptions, and play with what's conventional. Combined with my sense of humor. Oh, and also that I care so much—about my friends and people—to the point that it hurts. What a praise fest!

HOW WOULD SOMEONE WHO REALLY KNOWS YOU DESCRIBE YOUR WORST TRAITS? The same person I was thinking about above would probably say that I can be terribly self-absorbed. I constantly process myself, what I'm doing, who I am, often to the exclusion of being as loving as she deserves. I love so much, but I often don't show it enough because I assume my friends know how I feel about them.

DESCRIBE YOUR MOST EMBARRASSING MOMENT IN LIFE: Twenty minutes before the graduation ceremony at Simon's Rock, I wasn't in line because I was hooking up with an old roommate in my dorm room. It's all about closure. My whole family comes to the room looking for me. They knock, I pull the comforter over him, try to open the door from in bed, and fake a nap. Instead, I lost my balance, fell naked on the floor in the doorway. I look up at three rather scandalized faces. And all my mom can say is, "Slap a robe on that. It's starting." Teen hijinks.

DO YOU HAVE A BOYFRIEND OR GIRLFRIEND? Bad bad chapter. The last boy I was with fizzled—no, exploded—and I'm still recovering.

HOW IMPORTANT IS SEX TO YOU? It comes and goes, you know? Sex is an always omnipresent factor in my life. It fascinates me. At this point in my life, I haven't had many relationships that lasted beyond the six-month mark.

DESCRIBE YOUR FANTASY DATE: Burritos in the East Village, then chat at a cafe until about 11 p.m. Then we hit the bars until we go back and help each other get dressed to go out. Slap on the leather, platforms and glitter, unless the getting dressed leads to a detour... Looking fabulous, we travel to a Chelsea club, dance passionate and sweaty until 8 a.m., leave for breakfast, go home, shower, and cuddle into sleep.

OTHER THAN A BOYFRIEND OR GIRLFRIEND, WHO'S THE MOST IMPORTANT PERSON IN YOUR LIFE RIGHT NOW? My closest friend at law school—she is my sustenance in a sea of revolting corporate gloom.

IF YOU HAD TO DESCRIBE YOUR MOTHER BY DIVIDING HER PERSONALITY INTO TWO PARTS, HOW WOULD YOU DESCRIBE EACH PART? 1. Profoundly caring! 2. At the same time, she's not soft.

IF YOU HAD TO DESCRIBE YOUR FATHER BY DIVIDING HIS PERSONALITY INTO TWO PARTS, HOW WOULD YOU DESCRIBE EACH PART? 1. Brilliantly well-intentioned. 2. Withdrawn.

WHAT ARE YOUR THOUGHTS ON SEXUAL ORIENTATIONS? Straight people are great, though sometimes sadly lacking in the style department.

IF YOU HAD ALADDIN'S LAMP AND THREE WISHES, WHAT WOULD THEY BE? 1. Reform of a corrupt U.S. political system giving voice to the silenced, with 100% voter turnout. 2. Absorbing any book by touching it. 3. A bottomless bag of Prada clothes that changed with the season.

True Casting Confession:

Why I Should Be on The Real World.

JUSTiN: Let's talk about why you need me. Gosh, I guess, for two reasons. You know I'm a lovable and endearing, fun kind of guy but even more important, if you have a fire-and-brimstone kind of conservative evangelical quota for the show, I'm afraid you desperately need me as the antidote. You want someone to whip-smart 'em back into space. Let me be the token bleeding heart! That's what I'm good at. Plus, I might just fly out to Hawaii and meet the man of my dreams and marry him on the spot. That would be timely, wouldn't it? So, yeah, I'm ready for some fun, I'm ready to chill out. I'm ready to talk. I'm a smart guy, I'm wild, what more can I say.

THE

CREW

The Challenges of Filming The Real World-Hawaii

JORGE ALVES JR., CAMERAMAN: I've been a cameraman on *The Real World* since the Miami season. There was nudity on that season. Mike and Flora were running around without clothes all the time, but this was different. I work the night shift. On the first night, I got to work and the cast had already gone skinny-dipping! The truth is you have to desensitize yourself. To all of it—nudity and everything. That's what I was trained to do four seasons ago. It's been drilled into my head: keep shooting, don't interfere.

FILMING THE FIRST KISS

It was a battle among the camerapeople who was going to get Amaya and Colin's first onscreen kiss. And, yes, I got it. But, it comes with a story. Amaya and Colin were sitting on the sea wall. It was late out and they were just talking about their relationship. Colin said something like, "God, if the camera weren't in our face, maybe we'd feel more comfortable."

COLIN: YEAH, THAT WAS A REAL MOOD-BREAKER, WATCHING JORGE FALL INTO THE POOL. BUT IT WAS MAYBE THE FUNNIEST THING I'VE EVER SEEN.

FILMING THE DRINKING

Of course, that's difficult sometimes. Especially when you're scared a cast member is jeopardizing him or herself. Like with Ruthie. Watching her drink was difficult. And shooting her when she was drunk could get complicated. Thankfully, there was usually a cast member there to look out for her. If there hadn't been, we definitely would have had to step in. That second night when she got alcohol poisoning, we were really worried. But the cast was there to do the right thing.

CLOCKWISE: CREATOR, JON MURRAY; CREATOR, MARY-ELLIS BUNIM; TECK AND CREW MEMBERS ON FINAL DAY. CENTER: CAMERA MAN JORGE ALVES, JR.

So, nice guy that I am, I decide to give them a little space. I jump across the sea wall, onto the grass, and—although I don't realize it because I'm walking backward and still shooting—toward the pool. That's right, the pool. Next thing I know, I'm up to my head in water, still gripping a $100,000 camera. At first I was laughing, but then I was totally pissed. All that footage! The camera! I was freaking out. I recovered, though. And the production staff gave me a trophy!

So, of course, I missed that kiss. But I got them another time. I don't think they even realize when it was. I think they thought the camera was on Ruthie and I didn't see them sneaking off. But I did. I caught them making out. Finally.

True Confessions
of a **Real World-Hawaii Director**

Michelle Millard, Director: I went from being a *Real World* cast member reject (Yes, it's true!) to working in the casting department to actually directing *The Real World*. In the past couple of years I've lived in Seattle, Waikiki, and traveled in Mexico (for *Road Rules–Latin America*). I guess you could say I have the kind of personality that lends itself to this kind of lifestyle. Every day I'd come into my job having no idea what was going to happen next. One day I'm hiking down Manoa Falls in my bare feet trying to keep up with Ruthie and Justin; the next day I'm running along the beach at sunset following Colin and Amaya.

And if you're like me, and you've been doing this for a while, you don't have a real house. You move from rental to rental. All your stuff's in stor-

OF COURSE, THE CREW HAS ISSUES TOO. JUST LIKE THE CAST, WE MOVE TO A DIFFERENT CITY NOT KNOWING ANYBODY ELSE EXCEPT ONE ANOTHER. OUR SOCIAL LIVES AND WORK LIVES ARE COMPLETELY INTERTWINED. IT'S LIKE THE DYSFUNCTION IN THE CAST'S HOUSE EXTENDS ITSELF TO THE CREW.

age. You have no permanent address.

We have our own lives, of course, but we really do live vicariously through the cast. For example, we went to India and for me, it was the first time—that's a big deal. I got a trip I could never afford on my own. But I only got to see what the cast got to see. If a cast member decided to stay home and not go touring the countryside, that's what I had to do too. I'm not able to make any decisions, and I'm not traveling on my own merits. So, there are downsides. But, my God, it was India! I got to live on a train.

The truth is you actually get addicted to this kind of life. At least, I do. And I can never complain my job is boring. That's a lot more than most people can say!

The Real World-Hawaii and The Real World-Seattle

Matt Kunitz, Supervising Producer: I started out as a *Real World* fan. That's to say, I watched *The Real World—New York,* and was completely obsessed with what a great show it was. A friend mentioned a job opening at Bunim-Murray, and I became Jon and Mary-Ellis' assistant. For the L.A. season, I did everything. I was the cast contact; I was the production coordinator; I worked in the office during the day and on the set at night. The next season I worked on was San Francisco, moving up to associate producer. Then in London I was coordinating producer. Then I took a break. I still loved the show, though, so I came back to do the Seattle season as the producer.

There's a big difference between working in Seattle and Hawaii. Hawaii extended the Aloha spirit to our cast and crew 100%. In Seattle, that was definitely not the case. There was a "hipster elite" that didn't want us there. In Seattle we had to spend thousands of dollars on police to shield the house from passers-by. In Hawaii, the people were totally pleasant. No one cared.

But more important, the difference was the level of openness the Hawaii cast was willing to exhibit. This has been the most open cast we've ever had. They shared as much as they possibly could; they kept nothing from us. I'm not sure why that was. Yes, it had to do with the personalities involved, but it also had to do with some of our policies. While I never crossed the line and never interfered with the cast's lives, this season I was more willing to have "batphone" conversations with cast members, to deliver pep talks, to meet them in the park for short conversations. I wanted the cast to trust me and the rest of the crew. And I think they did.

I guess in a way I was reacting to Seattle. In Seattle there was a lot of paranoia, whispering and note passing. As a result, we were forced to use a lot of stealth footage—meaning we'd be shooting and the cast members wouldn't know it. We didn't want to disturb them, we wanted to have them act naturally. But we were sneaking around. This year, I wasn't willing to do that. We had a policy of anti-stealth. It was, "The camera's going to be in your face, so get used to it. You have no choice but to behave as you normally would."

I think it worked. Every year we're reinventing ourselves. We're constantly trying to make it better, to figure it all out.

THE REAL WORLD SEATTLE

JANET

The first time I saw myself on *The Real World*, I freaked out. It was awful. It's not like I haven't seen myself on video before. I've done newscasts for school. But I judged myself on how I spoke, on how I looked from one angle. Watching yourself on *The Real World* is a whole different thing. Seeing the way you wake up, your every gesture, it's suicide emotionally. We watched the casting special and the first episode at the premiere party, and I spent

World/Road Rules Challenge. I don't know what I would have done without it. It really helped me through that time. Being with other *Real Worlders*, people who'd been through the same experience, was invaluable. I clicked with those guys immediately. I had such a good time. I know it's crazy how incestuous we all are, how everyone dates everyone else. But you can't imagine how comfortable you feel. You don't have to worry that the person you're dating is just with you because of *The Real*

IT WASN'T UNTIL I WAS BY MYSELF THAT I ACTUALLY WATCHED—REALLY WATCHED—AN EPISODE OF THE REAL WORLD ALL THE WAY THROUGH. I GOT SO UPSET. I WAS LITERALLY POUNDING MY FISTS ON THE FLOOR OF MY PARENTS' HOUSE. ALL I COULD THINK WAS, "WHAT HAVE I GOTTEN MYSELF INTO? WHAT HAVE I DONE?"

the whole time trying not to look. Lindsay and I ran to the bathroom a couple of times—we were practically in tears.

Here was the first episode, and I already felt this way. Actually, it didn't get any easier—at least not for a while. There were twenty weeks when tapes would arrive in the mail, and I tell you, each time that tape arrived, my stomach would drop. Watching *The Real World* was the first time I saw how people really saw me. And my self-esteem crumbled. I went through this paranoid stage. I couldn't talk about it. I wouldn't let my friends talk about it. I thought that anyone new I met was interested in me only because of the show.

Thank God I was invited to go on *The Real*

World. Going out with Jason was great for me. (See page Janet and Jason.) I haven't gone out with anyone else since. The truth is that, at this point, the only people I feel like I can date are people from the past or from the shows or the crew. Anyone I meet now, I feel like they won't like me as me. They won't base their opinion of me on just what I give them. They have all this background material. That summer after the *Challenge,* I was back in Los Angeles hanging out with other *Real World* and *Road Rules* kids: Jason, Kalle, Syrus, Vince, Devon... they were there. It's so relaxing to be around them, it's almost dangerous. You want to just use your *Real World* status, make it the thing that most identifies

TOTAL CRINGE:

Every shot of me waking up in the morning. The way I say, "I have a secret boyfriend." How I act on the bungee jump during the *Challenge*. I can't believe I had an anxiety attack!

WHAT YOU DON'T SEE:

How much money we rack up on our credit cards. You get so bored, you have all this free time, and you have to get away from the house as much as possible. You only work eighteen hours a week, so you end up spending a lot of cash. I was totally maxed out.

FAVORITE MOMENT:

When Lindsay's reading from that sex book and she purrs like a kitty. Ha ha.

LEAST FAVORITE MOMENT:

There's this shot of me on the phone with my dad. My face is all crinkled up. I look like a newborn walrus.

FASHION FLUB:

That dress I was wearing during the "Irene leaves" episode. It's a long tank dress, and it is not flattering.

you. There are enough perks, enough tasty things, you want to use it, stick with it, feel like the recognition actually means something. But I don't feel like I earned that recognition. And, after a while, when it was time to go home, I realized that what I want to do is move on, get back to my old goals—which are still my current goals: to graduate school and go into journalism, and just be happy. Once you're on *The Real World,* people's expectations of you change. And you internalize those expectations: if you become anything less than a movie star, you're pathetic.

So I started trying to get back to normal. Being at school is good, though it's not always the easiest. On campus, people are always looking at me. Not to mention the fact that I had a stalker who kept bothering my family. I'm ready to get beyond college. I've been all over the place. You wouldn't believe how into the show some people are. I get asked about the Mount Everest incident the most, the time I fainted from smoking a cigarette. I would

FAMILY FLAK:

I was just expecting to disappoint my parents. But in the end, through all the hard times in the aftermath, they were the most supportive of anyone. They hate how much I smoke on the show, but that's the worst it's gotten. That said, I didn't tell them when the *Challenge* episodes were airing, because I didn't think they'd want to see that *Playboy* Mansion show. (You know, the one with me and Jason...)

MOST HOW-IT-WAS:

I feel like the shows really represented Irene's departure well, what it was like to be around her. She was pure chaos. I feel guilty when I look back at the Irene episodes, like maybe I should have tried to help more. But it was so difficult. And you can see that.

LEAST HOW-IT-WAS:

Nathan and Stephanie's relationship. They have so much more love between them than it seems. She's much more caring and loving than she came off.

DIRTY LAUNDRY:

Lindsay would always go into the bathroom to put on her makeup, so the cameras didn't see. She wanted to keep up the front of having a natural look!

just like to clear that up: I fainted because of the altitude, not from a cigarette. I fainted because I'm from Chicago, the flattest of flatlands. And, you know, everyone was smoking up there. Everyone except Rebecca and Lindsay. I just got unlucky.

I also get asked about Justin a lot. That's another thing I'd like to clear up. Justin wasn't the big romance it looked like. The truth is I was never planning on doing anything that much with him. I'm not okay with public displays of affection, and *The Real World* just takes it to a whole new level. So Justin and I just weren't a big deal. But, oh my God, I looked like such a bitch. Ditching him like that. I think he was really pissed off. He got a lot of s**t at the market. He looked like such a puppy dog!

It wasn't until after the first run of the series that I was actually able to watch the shows on television. It was a marathon that got me back into it. The whole aftermath has taught me a lot. At first, I wanted to come off perfect. But I realize I've got issues the same as anyone else. *"Take the good, take the bad"* is how I see it now.

My favorite episode of the season was the goodbye show. We were all so afraid about leaving and going home, and I think that's captured really well. We'd just had this totally solid experience, and we had no idea what was going to happen next.

CAME OFF AS:

"The Asian girl." I obviously add to the rainbow of the show. I represent strong family values. I think people think I'm high maintenance—like when Stephen and I are fighting over makeup.

SPEED DIAL:

I keep in touch with Nathan and David, and talk to them often. Lindsay—I speak to her about once a month. Stephen and I play phone tag. I think he's going through a really hard time. Rebecca and I haven't spoken. And Irene, no, we're not in touch.

SHOCKER:

I never saw Stephen wearing that wig! And I didn't know anything about his fight with Aubie. And I had no idea how stupid David looked having his shirt off all the time! Oh, and the fight with Kira, my God...I saw his bashed-up knuckles but I wasn't prepared for that scene.

BIGGEST REGRET:

Having relationships on camera!

JANET:

Of all the *Real World* seasons, the one I'd seen the most was Boston. The way Jason was on the Boston season—trendy but preppy—he really reminded me of my hometown boys. He was a lot like my old boyfriend, actually. But I never thought anything would happen between us. Honestly. In fact, the first time I met him, I thought he was a total jerk. It was at the premiere party—he was working at Bunim/Murray Productions at the time—that I first met him. You knew he thought he was the s**t. He had on these really trendy dark-blue jeans and his hair was all dyed blond. He was working a glam-rock look, and that's not my thing. So when I found out he was going to be on *The Challenge,* I didn't even think anything of it. Anyway, the trip was only two weeks long, so I didn't think romance would really figure into it.

Jason was kind of flirting with me at first. I told him straight up I thought he was an asshole. I mean, at the premiere party, two girls told me they were seeing him—and then who knows about Timber? He kept persisting, and I kept holding back. We were four days into the trip, and Nate said to me, "Jason likes you." I was like, "Who doesn't he like?"

But I changed my mind. I guess it was this really romantic drive we took—without the cameras. We were just relaxing, sitting up in the front seat, and I thought to myself, "Oh, he's cute." There were still things that really irked me. He's so high maintenance, and as I said, I usually like guy guys, rustic ones. But despite that, I started to like him. We had really good talks. He's so in tune with feminine emotions; he's really sincere.

JANET & JASON

THE FIRST KISS

The first night we kissed was when we were staying in this hotel in Santa Monica. Montana and Noah were wrestling in the living room, so the cameras stayed on them. We snuck into this little side room. He put his hand on my cheek—of course he'd be a two-hands-around-the-face kind of guy and of course I love that—and I put my arms around his neck and it was a really nice deep-lipped kiss. I remember thinking his lips were really soft. It wasn't premeditated, but it wasn't a surprise either. It just kind of happened. It was great, but it didn't go any further. After the whole Justin thing, I didn't want anything to get on camera. So I pulled away. I talked to Jason and I told him I didn't want a relationship—especially with cameras monitoring it.

But I was falling for him. By the time we got to Vegas, the crew people were hounding me. They really don't have much footage of me and Jason together. That's because we were sneaking around. In Vegas, we were hanging out, being a little more intimate, but it was all secret. One time we snuck into the stairwell of the Hard Rock Cafe, and were totally kissing. The camera guy just missed us.

It wasn't until the *Playboy* Mansion that things got, well....There was an open bar and Montana, Neil, Jason, and I were all hanging around. All of a sudden Jason and I decided to get up and leave. We went off to this little area behind the hedges to be alone. Of course, it had never occurred to us that there were security cameras everywhere. That's how we got caught!

The *Challenge* ended, and Nate, Kalle, and I went to stay with Jason in L.A. at his and Vince's

(Road Rules 4) place for a week. It was really romantic...the four of us. It was stupid *Sweet Valley High* kind of stuff: beaches and cafes and lovin'. When I had to leave to go back to Seattle for a few days [to host a music festival called "Endfest" with Lindsay and David], we decided that that would be it. But then we were apart and I was really missing him. He paid for half my ticket and I came back for two weeks. Those two weeks were amazing. It was really passionate and intense. I really fell for him and him for me—I can say that with confidence. I really had no reason to trust him, but I just really wanted to. He has that effect on women.

I went home for a week only to come back to L.A. again. That's how into this guy I was. We were inseparable. At the MTV Music Video Awards, all these musicians—the bassist from No Doubt, and that guy Rob from Matchbox 20—asked me to hang out, but I blew them all off for Jason. I was so consumed; I hadn't felt that intense before. I was truly enjoying the moment.

By the time I started back at school, I decided we needed to end it. I couldn't concentrate on my life and, truthfully, Timber was still part of the picture. A big part. I don't want to go into it more than that. We just needed to end it. I still consider us tight. And I value what we had. Being with him rekindled my faith in love.

JASON:

Janet is one of the coolest girls I've ever met. She's beautiful. She's stunning. She's incredibly sexy. And she's really sweet. She's nice to everyone. When Bunim/Murray asked me to do *The Real World/Road Rules Challenge*, I had a hunch she might be coming too. I starting tuning in to the Seattle shows, thinking, "Damn, I hope that Janet girl comes."

The connection between us was instant. I don't know about her, but for me there were sparks with-in the first couple of hours. She's just got this energy about her. She's an amazing listener. She's like a sponge, soaking everything up.

One night I was talking to Nathan, and I told him I was really digging on Janet. He told me she'd said the same thing about me. He was like our cupid. That night, we kissed at the Shangri-La Hotel. It's true that we kept our relationship under wraps. Janet didn't want it on camera; she didn't want her love life scrutinized. Me, I didn't care; I wasn't the least bit embarrassed. Maybe it was because she'd just come off the show that she was so nervous. I was over it. Timber and I had broken up, so I wasn't worried about that. I just didn't care. I didn't even mind when we finally got busted at the *Playboy* Mansion. But let me just say this: had we gone public earlier, they would have had a lot more footage.

We were never really boyfriend and girlfriend, but we had a great time together. After the *Challenge*, she came out to visit a few times. It was a blast. Coffee and cigarettes, that was our ritual. We'd go down to the beach or go to the movies. Or we'd just sit around naked at my house, making coffee and smoking cigarettes and just yap-yapping about things.

Now we see each other every few months. We're still tight. It's all good every time we get together. But I miss her. Probably more as a friend than as a lover, though she was that too. I know we needed to part ways because of distance. But I still think of her. Not in a "wish you were here" kind of way. It's more like: "God, that was a good thing."

MARY-ELLIS BUNIM:

Janet and Jason—what an interesting couple! They're a mass of contrasts and contradictions. Janet's very right-brained and Jason's definitely left-brained. But they share intellect, sensuality, and a curiosity about other people. They could learn a lot from each other.

DAVID

et me put it this way: for me, the last day of *The Real World* was a lie. On-screen, I was saying these big good-byes. But in spirit, I was gone. When we were at the airport, I was thinking that I wouldn't see these people for a year. I was thinking that maybe I'd just stay in Africa, travel around. The way I was feeling was just, "Bye, see you." We were six people, six really cool kids, but it was just time for me to go. I wanted to see my family, get strong, and move on.

A week after the show, I went to Morocco. I was there for three months. The whole time I was in Morocco, I talked to three people: my mom, my

hear that it had been on television...I was taken aback. You know, I still haven't seen that episode. It'd be too painful.

When I got home, there were ten overnight packages from Bunim/Murray waiting for me. In the beginning I watched the show alone, but then I started to watch it with buddies. The bars in Boston have *Real World* nights on Tuesdays. I was in a bar when the Kira and me episode came on, and I just gave the bartender a look. He turned it right off. You just don't go there with me, and he knew it. Then again, there was another kid who had the nerve to come up to me and imitate how I scream at Kira. He was in my face,

THERE I WAS ACTING LIKE I LIKED REBECCA, FLIRTING WITH LINDSAY. I'M NOT GOING TO SAY THERE WASN'T SEXUAL TENSION IN THE HOUSE. COME ON. YOU'VE GOT A BUNCH OF TWENTY-SOMETHINGS IN THE HOUSE AND GIRLS THAT ARE PRETTY—OF COURSE, THERE'S GOING TO BE TENSION. BUT, PLEASE! I DIDN'T THINK IT WAS LIKE THAT. OR MAYBE IT WAS...

mentor, Tom, and Kira. I asked them not to talk about the show with me. I didn't want to know anything about it. Basically they kept to their end of the deal, though Tom told me a few times that he was disappointed in me, that I wasn't coming off like I had class. Kira wouldn't tell me details, but she would warn me, "It's not good, honey." She told me about the truck scene where I bashed my knuckles on the dashboard. That was a shock. Neither of us knew we were being filmed when we were in that car screaming at each other. So to

yelling, "It's killin' me, Kira!" I threw such a punch at him. I missed him. If I hadn't, he would have died. I hit a wall, instead. The kid still started crying.

You know why I still haven't watched that show? Because I know enough not to. It was so emotional that night. I really didn't want it to be filmed. In fact, I broke the rules so that it wouldn't be filmed. When Kira called me from the gas station, I ran out of the house, took off my mike, wrapped it up in a T-shirt, and got into the car. I had no idea the mike would still pick up our conversation, and I had no idea that the crew had tracked us down. We were

MOST HOW-IT-WAS:
Stephen's behavior. That was portrayed exactly how it was. Anger management seemed comical to me, but hopefully it helped him.

LEAST HOW-IT-WAS:
Either the Kira situation or Stephanie. She comes off awfully, but she's the bomb.

out on the waterfront near a construction site, completely isolated—or so I thought. The camera crew had actually caught up with us, parked five hundred feet from our car, and turned their lights off. One of the camera guys hid in a ditch just behind the car, filming as I split my f**king knuckles open and Kira slapped me in the face. What they got on that night was purely human.

I've grown pretty detached from the experience. Now I kind of enjoy my post–*Real World* status. I know when I talk, I affect people. I talk about the human dimension of the experience, and self-respect. I've learned how to project energy to a crowd, and I think that's a good thing.

I graduated from Virginia Military Institute (VMI) in the spring. I wish I'd had Nathan by my side, but he's a grown man who can make his own decisions. He wants to be an entertainer. As for me, I have to go where my passions lie. I'm going to Paris for a year or two to study at L'Ecole Polytechnique, and after that I'd like to go to graduate school. I don't speak such great French, but I plan on learning more. Kira and I couldn't deal with the long distance between us, so I'm viciously single at the moment. I can just leave without strings.

FASHION FLUB:

Turtleneck and a slick-back. That's all you have to say.

SPEED DIAL:
I talk to Janet all the time, Lindsay pretty often, and Nathan pretty often. I've talked to Rebecca once or twice. I never talk to Stephen. Irene and I have actually hung out a lot. She's totally great, different from how she was on the show— funny, vibrant, sexy, not cuckoo. She's f**king smart. Yeah, she's watched the shows. She's bitter, but she's detached.

TOTAL CRINGE:

In the clip show, they show me coming out of the hot tub, naked, with the pool cover draped over me. Terrible.

FAMILY FLAK:
My family was troubled by the Kira incident. They've never seen me so confused. On a less serious note, my mother was mad at me for showing my penis on TV. I really got a lashing for that. "That was no class, David," is what she told me.

CAME OFF AS:

A goofball. I wish my other side had come out more, the more serious, thoughtful side. I'm not as much of a comedian or a drama queen.

FAME

Everywhere I go, I'm stopped. It's amazing. But, it can also be a source of aggravation. Women come on to me just because I'm that guy on *The Real World.* Cheesy agents call me telling me I'm the next big thing. People think they can violate me just because I'm on a reality-based TV show. I don't want to sound like a cracker, but I never realized how powerful this medium could be.

DESERVED MORE PLAY:

Me and my friends hanging out. I had five people visit. We had the greatest time. Had they shown us hanging out together, we probably would have gotten movie contracts.

BIGGEST REGRET:

That Kira was part of the show. Actually, f**k that. I don't regret anything.

FAVORITE MOMENT:

We're in Nepal, and Stephen's fighting with Janet at a dinner that was being made for us. I scream at him: "Listen, they're making us a kick-ass meal." I loved that. My mother loved that too. She was like, "That's my David." I also like the moment when Irene, with raspberry lips and drunk on red wine, was in the hot tub imitating a pigeon. She's so funny.

LEAST FAVORITE MOMENT:

Me and Kira in the truck, that's the lowest of the low.

The Real World was seriously a good experience for me—even with its dark side. I grew a lot. I made some great friends. The most profound effect it had on my life was that it took away my anonymity. Of course, where it counts, no one really cares—like at VMI or at home. After Paris, I don't know what I'm going to do. But I know there's a lot out there. Chalk up another experience, and move on.

NATHAN

When *The Real World–Seattle* began airing, the phone started ringing. We've got a short shelf life, us *Real World*–ers; there's a new cast just around the bend. That's why I decided to take advantage of this time. I took a leave from the Virginia Military Istitute (VMI), transferred to Virginia Commonwealth, moved to Richmond, and decided to concentrate on acting and modeling. I hear there are rumors that David was furious at me for leaving VMI, but they're totally unfounded. He understands what I'm trying to do, that I'm not making a mistake. VMI's a perfect place, and eventually I am going to finish up there. But right now, I really feel I have to do this.

A lot of modeling agencies have

ing around, it's really embarrassing. I would watch the show each week with my friends here in Richmond, Stephanie included. We'd wait for it to come on, like we were about to watch 90210. To me, though, it always felt like a home video. It is weird flipping through the channels and coming upon my face all huge on the screen. And hearing my voice really threw me. In the first episode, I say, "Damn, we have under-the-pier lights!" I never realized I sounded like such a redneck. And it's true what they say: the camera definitely does put some extra weight on you. People are always surprised when they see me, like they thought I was some big burly guy or something.

A difficult thing about watching *The Real World* was seeing how

MOSTLY IT'S YOUNG GIRLS WHO COME UP TO ME, BUT SOME-TIMES PARENTS ASK ME FOR AUTOGRAPHS. "MY DAUGHTER'S NOT GOING TO BELIEVE I SAW YOU!" THEY'LL SAY. MORE PEOPLE WATCH THE SHOW THAN I EVER THOUGHT WOULD. IT'S INSANE TO THINK THAT ALL THESE PEOPLE CARE ENOUGH ABOUT MY LIFE TO TUNE IN EACH WEEK.

been calling me; telling me I have a good look. I haven't signed with anyone. I did get contacted to do a Guess Jeans ad. Am I going to be next Anna Nicole Smith? I hope not. I'm also doing two independent films. In one, I'm playing a French soldier. The other is a Civil War film.

Since the show, it's been crazy. Everywhere I go in public, I'm recognized. In bookstores, just walk-

much I drank. Watching myself as I walked home in a drunk stupor with Rebecca following me—seeing that really did make me wise up a bit. I was drinking really heavily at the time. I look like a jackass. It took actually seeing that show to realize how much of a jackass drinking made me be.

I've only seen each show once, maybe twice. I don't like to watch them over and over again. I

would feel stuck on myself. I just really don't want my friends to think that about me. I didn't want them to think I'd be all stuck up and stuff. I definitely was different, though. After living with six people and going through all we went through, I did feel like a better person. But that was as different as I wanted them to think I'd gotten.

As for Stephanie, well, things have changed. We're not together at the moment, though we're still working on it. Immediately after the show, things got hard. She picked me up at the airport. I told her as soon as possible about having kissed another girl, though at the time I didn't know they were going to show it on TV. I begged her for forgiveness, and we got back together. We went on vacation with her family to Bermuda. I was there when I got a call from Bunim/Murray Productions to do *The Real World/Road Rules Challenge.* I knew it was going to be a problem, but I had to accept it. How could I miss that opportunity? There was no way I wasn't going to go. Stephanie was shocked. "You're leaving...again?" She was pissed. "Why don't you just not call me for two weeks?" she told me.

So we broke it off again. And the truth is, being on *The Challenge* was exactly what I needed. Janet and I really needed to meet people from other seasons. We hadn't yet dealt with the spotlight, and it was like we were rookies. Those guys really helped prepare us. It was just some unbelievable bonding.

And, then, of course, there was Kalle *(Road Rules-Islands)*. Mentally, I was attracted to Kalle instantly. The first conversation we had was about my father. We talked about the parallel relationships we'd had going into the shows. And, yeah, in Vegas we danced a lot. But, you know, it's Vegas. What else can you do? Kalle and I didn't actually get together on the show. We kissed for the first time after taping stopped, when we were both in Los Angeles hanging out.

But Stephanie and I still got back together. I guess you can say it's on-and-off for us. I wouldn't say that *The Real World* broke us up. It's just that both of us changed so much. I'll always love her, though.

I'm working hard now. It's not like I don't know this is a risk. Please...actors are a dime a dozen. But I'm going for it anyway, going where the wind takes me.

MOST HOW IT WAS:
Janet. She's always been the same wonderful person.

LEAST HOW IT WAS:
David and Kira. David was going through a lot more turmoil than it seemed.

FAME:
At the MTV Video Music Awards, this girl fell to my feet screaming my name. Wow. I've signed everything. Pieces of paper. Books. Explicit body parts. There's so much fan mail, I can't respond to it all. The main question people ask is: "Are you still with Stephanie?" Or: "Irene's voice, was it really as grating as it sounds?" I get a lot of mail from married couples with inspirational advice for me and Stephanie.

SPEED DIAL:
I talk to Janet the most. Then David. Then Lindsay and Stephen. I've run into Rebecca in Richmond a couple of times. I've tried to call Irene, but I wouldn't say I've made huge efforts.

SHOCKER:
Irene's confessional when she was stuttering about cleaning the house. That was a huge eye-opener for me. Her behavoir was just as it seemed on the show—abrupt. To me it seemed like it happened overnight.

TOTAL CRINGE:
When we were in Nepal and I screamed, "Oh my God, there's a monkey just sitting on a rock." People always repeat that to me when they see me.

he first time I saw *The Real World–Seattle*, I cried. It's like seeing your life through a different person's eyes. It's like you're watching a nature show, only you're the little animal on-screen.

Which is not to say I don't consider *The Real World* one of the best experiences for me. I do. It was the best learning experience; but it was incredibly painful. I grew up in a bubble, very secluded. My whole life, I felt I needed to overcome where I was from. But, in Seattle, once I got there and the bubble popped, I didn't feel freedom. I felt alone the airport. They had all of my favorite kinds of ice cream with them. I was so happy.

But after a few days, I felt like I had ants in my pants. I had this urgent feeling, this, "What should I do? What should I do?" The reason *The Real World* is dangerous is that fast-paced cameras in your face become normal. It's like abnormal becomes normal. Well, coming home, having a regular life, though it was wonderful, also felt unnatural. Not having cameras in my face felt strange. It was very *The Truman Show*.

Watching the show was terrifying and fascinat-

> AFTER THE SHOW, ALL I WANTED TO DO IS DIVE BACK INTO THE BUBBLE. AS IT TURNS OUT, I WAS WRONG ABOUT THE BUBBLE! I LOVE THE BUBBLE! THAT'S WHAT I MOST GOT FROM THE SHOW: AN APPRECIATION FOR THE BUBBLE. I WAS SO EXCITED TO GET BACK TO MY LIFE, TO HAVE THIS BEHIND ME.

and vulnerable. I have a very gentle nature and I was in a situation with people who are different, who don't exactly mesh with sensitive people. I would call my best friend or my mom and be like, "Help me." I'd go to the confessional and cry. I didn't feel like anyone was out for me. In my life, I have very few friends, but the friends I have I take very seriously. They're hard-core friendships with a lot of give and take. I missed out on that on *The Real World*. I didn't have any allies. I didn't have anyone to support me. I didn't have a soul mate.

Coming home was like stepping into a warm bath. My mom and my boyfriend picked me up at

ing all at once. It took a while to get used to it. People really don't want to understand the editing process. They want to think that things actually happened just as they look on TV. Watching an early episode, the way it was edited, makes it look like I was blowing David off. Well, I remember it differently. But, watching the show, I found myself believing what was on the television screen—as opposed to relying on my own memory. The editing made me change how I remembered things. People want to believe what they see and read—even if they know better. That's so fascinating to me.

SHOCKER:

Most of the show surprised me. I didn't know anything about Lindsay and David, Janet and Nathan, Kira and David. Actually most of the show was an eye-opener. I live in my own little world.

FAVORITE MOMENT:

Watching us ride elephants. When David tries to show me his anatomy and I say, "No thanks." That's one of my favorite moments. My family was like, "Yeah, that's so you." My best friend was like, "That's Rebecca."

LEAST FAVORITE MOMENT:

I can't stand seeing the slap. Oh, and in the Sir Mix-a-lot episode, I say something like, "Music is the outpouring of my soul." I screamed over that so that my parents couldn't hear it. How dorky! I felt like such an idiot.

FAMILY FLAK:

My family was really happy with the show, my grandfather especially. He's this high-powered New York attorney, who became just addicted to the show. He said that he couldn't believe I put up with those people, but I came off great.

FASHION FLUB:

There's this quick shot of me Roller-blading with Janet. I'm wearing my boyfriend's boxer briefs and a tank top. Horrifying. My butt was totally sagging in those briefs. But I can also say I'm proud of being seen in my "Don't Mess with Texas" T-shirt.

DESERVED MORE PLAY:
My friendship with Irene. There was so much more to it.

DESERVED LESS PLAY:
The stuff about my being intimidated by men—embarrassing!

What was really weird about watching the show was seeing the interviews. I hate that these six people are allowed to say *anything* about me they want. And you know what? They say wrong things, a lot of them. I feel like I never lost that sense of decorum, that sense that you should perhaps keep unfounded opinions to yourself, that you don't have the license to say whatever it is you think

at that moment. The truth is, I feel weird even talking about this stuff.

My boyfriend doesn't watch the show. I don't want him to see it. That episode with David, no one would want to see that; it would make him feel vulnerable to see me in that position. I don't think he likes seeing me as an entertainer. It's hard enough for him that I'm in a band. But for him to see me on the show, that's too much. How I seem on the show is different from how I seem to him in real life. I'm more academic, more analytical. Of course, he hadn't been stoked about my doing *The Real World* in the first place. That's why I hid him; I wanted to keep him safe, not expose him. I signed the contract; He didn't. That was the hardest thing about doing *The Real World*—not talking to him. We're still together; we're in a completely committed relationship.

Being back at school is great, though it's weird to have people recognize me for *The Real World* and not just for being a student. The worst is people looking at you and then looking away. It

SPEED DIAL:

I've spoken with David once or twice. Stephen called me, but I haven't called him back. I've run into Nathan in Richmond. I've spoken with Irene, though not recently. I know it's weird we're not more in touch, when we were actually really close. But it doesn't feel normal. All we'd talk about is *The Real World,* and Irene's so negative about it. I can't keep focusing on the bad side. I talk to the REI guide, Kelsey; we got really close. I talk to Martin, the sound guy. There were friendships that came out of it, but for whatever reason they were from behind the scenes.

MODELING

Just after the casting special aired, a modeling agency called me—IMG in New York. I signed with them, and I did a catalog for Abercrombie & Fitch. It was shot by Bruce Weber. Modeling is a means of making a lot of money for graduate school. But that's it. I'd like to go to law school, maybe, but it's really expensive.

I signed with a talent agency, too. Acting, I think it's fun, but I'm by no means a natural. My body seems to not do what my mind tells it to.

made me paranoid at first. I couldn't figure out why people were looking at me. Was it *The Real World* or was something really wrong with me?

I'm in my third year of school. I'm studying all the time. I also have a band called With Rebecca. We have a CD out. We're playing coffeehouses. I've gotten a lot of e-mails about the single I did for Sir Mix-a-lot. I started writing lyrics. I love it. I love collaborating. With school and music, it's hard for me to get away.

I don't really see the other cast members that much. We were in the real world under unreal circumstances. Friendships born of that, I'm not sure if they can survive.

MOST HOW-IT-WAS:

Nepal. I get chills watching those episodes. That's when I realized I was overly dependent on my boyfriend. Watching it brings it all back.

LEAST HOW-IT-WAS:

Stephanie's behavior. People think Nathan was going out with the biggest jerk and that's so not true.

TOTAL CRINGE:

Stage diving and singing Joan Osborne. I felt like such a nerd. I was totally sober. My friends saw that and thought I'd gone insane.

FAME:

I've had mainly good experiences with fans. Overall, people from the University of Virginia are really cool about it, though I hate when people scream, "You're that chick from *The Real World!*" Of course, there are a few psychos. Some guy followed me into my apartment once. I had to change my e-mail and my phone. And once someone accused me of being mean to David. I was really stunned when I was at Long John Silver and this eighty-year-old screamed "Rebecca!" Wow. Usually I'm polite, but when people ask for my autograph, I find it too embarrassing. I'm like, "Dude, what is this worth?"

CAME OFF AS:

Introspective, innocent, and nice. I wasn't upset with how I came off at all. I felt it was complimentary. I consider myself innocent; I can be naive—call it ignorant, call it what you will—it's just that I choose not to surround myself with negative things.

"Don't watch *The Real World* when you see it on TV. Turn the channel." That was the pact I made with myself. And I kept to it...for a while. Watching the shows reminded me of who I was then. I was young, maybe only a year younger than I am now, but the difference is amazing. I'm so much wiser now. I've done a lot of growing up since the show started airing. I had to.

Immediately after the show, I was worried all the time about what was going to happen; I was going through a difficult time. That last month on the show was really hard for me, so when I got home, I didn't keep in touch with anyone. I disassociated myself from the cast. Maybe I talked to Rebecca once. I watched the tapes they sent me, of course, but I kept a low profile.

We had to go to New York to film the clip show. That was the day before the "Irene slap"

childish then. I had so many little fights. I spent all this time focusing on how different we were; I forgot about the things we had in common.

At Berkeley, I'm taking anthropology and sociology courses. They've taught me a lot about being on *The Real World*. The best was in sociology, learning about the "scripted universe." In a scripted universe, you're not really what you are, you're what you audition to be. Everyone has an assumed role, from which it's incredibly difficult to break out. That's what *The Real World* was like.

I watched the "slap" episode with my friend Jigme. He's one of my best friends. He's from Tibet and he's a really peaceful, collected guy. He was like my guardian angel when I got back home. He told me not to take it so hard, and to remember that compassion manifests good karma. He laughed when he saw it. "You didn't even slap her hard." Actually, that's what most peo-

PEOPLE NEED TO UNDERSTAND THAT THERE'S INTENSE PRESSURE IN THE HOUSE. YOU NEVER TRULY FEEL CALM. YOU CAN'T LISTEN TO MUSIC. YOU CAN'T WATCH TV. IT'S NOT EVER REAL AT ALL. THAT'S BECAUSE CAMERAS CHANGE EVERYTHING. JUST WATCH ED TV.

episode aired. I was freaking out, and being with my castmates compounded it. It just all came back to me. But they were great. Lindsay hugged me and comforted me, told me, "You're with friends. You're a great person." It was then that I realized some really good things had come out of the experience. I started to miss it, to remember it in a positive light. It took me a while to get nostalgic for Seattle, to have affection for my time there. A lot of healing had to be done until I was able to enjoy the episodes. Let's just say this: Therapy rules.

I watch those episodes and realize I was so

ple said. "This girl wasn't acting right," is what most people tell me. Now, I'm not saying it was right to slap her. It was definitely a lapse in judgment. But I don't know if I had to feel as bad about it as I did. In that interview room the directors were socializing me, trying to make me feel it was the worst thing possible. I'm not saying there was ever any pride in hitting someone. But in the end, watching it on TV, I just had to laugh at myself. I was like, "Stephen, you're so crazy. The girl was already leaving!" You know, I had to go to anger management, but David and Nathan, they're the ones with

FAVORITE MOMENT:

David was trying to get with Rebecca, and I'm lying in my bed reading a book and laughing. That was the best moment to me. All this funny stuff was going on, but it wasn't often you could sit back and enjoy it.

LEAST FAVORITE MOMENT:

Picking up the phone when Lindsay's mom called her to say that Bill died. I was totally blasted. She'd been so introverted, and to see everything just ooze out of her. I've never lost anyone like that. Knowing that he was there three weeks before...God.

SPEED DIAL:

I speak to Lindsay, Janet, Rebecca, and David. I don't talk to Nathan. When I need him for business reasons, I'll call him. And, yes, I did talk to Irene. It was like three months after the show, when I first called her. She was not responsive at first, and didn't answer any of the messages I left with her parents. But finally, she called me back. She was like, "Oh, Stephen." I told her, "You know, Irene, we could have been best friends." And then I apologized for what happened. I told her I learned a lot from her. After the apology, we started talking. Our main topic was "the process." I thank Irene now. I learned a lot. I did her wrong, but we moved on.

DESERVED MORE PLAY:

I volunteered at a soup kitchen for AIDS patients. And I wish they'd shown more of me out with my friends.

DESERVED LESS PLAY:

The slap. Of course I'm going to say that.

LOSING MY RELIGION:

For anyone who saw the casting special, I guess I should let them know I've abandoned my Judaism. I've no religion. When I came back here, no one was nice to me. Truth was, Judaism was really forced on me. I felt like I had to convert. But after Nepal, I really believe that everyone's different. I'm more about Taoism now. Really it's circumstances that change your life. It's only you that you can rely on, not organized religion.

bigger problems. You saw them get into a fight too.

I met Gladys, the girl who got kicked off *Road Rules-Latin America*—at the premiere party. She got kicked out for assaulting Abe, supposedly. I wanted to offer both her and Abe support. It's really hard to live with the stigma of being kicked off, or almost kicked off. And, Abe, he didn't come off so well on the show. I figured he was probably getting a lot of flak. So, I gave him some hard-earned advice: "Live your life. Don't do it for anyone else." That's what I've learned in my life after *The Real World*.

DIRTY LAUNDRY:

Nathan deserves to be straight-up dogged for quitting school. He got to Seattle, said VMI and Stephanie were the most important things to him. Yeah, right. I just want to say to that guy, "Nathan, you're not a celebrity. You're on *The Real World*. That means nothing." We're like people on commercials—bad commercials—or on cheap public service announcements.

FASHION FLUB:

Dress to kill, but if you kill in the process, so be it. The outfit I'm wearing when I slap Irene, that was the worst. I had on these pants we called "the sex pants" because they've got all these holes in the ass and crotch areas. We also called them "the Gimme Some pants." I threw them away. And then I was wearing this white polyester shirt that's completely ridiculous. It's all Seventies. And then I had on what I call my "slap me hat." That's because I can't wear that hat without thinking of the slap. Recently, I wore it out and didn't feel bad. That was a big step for me.

MODELING:

Before I got on the show I was kind of working, doing a Joe Boxer campaign. Now I work pretty often. I did a CK bus billboard. That was kind of amazing. To see me flying past on a bus! I've flown to Europe, traveled in Rome and Florence and Paris. I met Antonio Sabato and Kate Moss. Modeling is not what I want to do forever, but it's making me a lot of money. But I'm sick of dieting and starving. I'd like to eat doughnuts again. So, I've decided I'm going to go pre-law. With all the networking I've done, I think I should go into entertainment law.

As for my family, while the show was airing I stayed away from my mom. I was scared to talk to her. One of the main reasons I was avoiding her was the episode about my past, the one where I talk about having been mistreated. Watching that was really hard for my mom. When I went back home, she accused me of embarrassing her on national television. "Yeah," I said, "but it was all true. And it's time we're finally up-front about it. I don't have a positive relationship with you, and I want one."

Now, after the show and our separation, we're the best we've ever been. *The Real World* let me reflect on our history and be honest about it. That was the biggest thing that came out of *The Real World:* I admitted that I was mistreated. I saw why things weren't playing out right. And you know what? I've been on top of the world since: loving life, seeing stuff for what it is, and being good to myself. I see myself in both negative and positive lights. I've forgiven myself for the bad stuff. And as far as what other people think, I've decided just to let it all go.

The best thing you can do is kiss life. I stop and kiss life everyday.

MOST HOW-IT-WAS:

Nathan's story line. Everything he did was preprogrammed; except his alcohol drinking. He drank to get drunk. He drank during the day and at work. He's going to be so pissed, but whatever. If he needs me sometime, he'll still call me.

LEAST HOW-IT-WAS:

Irene's behavior. She was acting strangely for a lot longer than it seemed. There were incidents at work, in the studio, on the phone, that were pretty out of the ordinary.

I got fan mail from Christian people preaching nonviolence; I got death threats. People come up to me on the street and scream. They'll say something like, "Man, that was a phat-ass slap!" "That was the phattest *Real World* moment." My response? "Thank you, but don't try it at home."

It can be hard being at school during all this. *The Daily Cal,* our newspaper, wrote that I was really stuck-up. They called me "Mr. Hollywood at Berkeley." Sometimes students stop me on the street and if I have to go to class, they get mad. Of all people, they should understand!

Yes, people ask me all the time if I'm gay. But I've been hearing that since high school. If you're a young African-American who is not hip-hop or thuggish, you get that. I'm actually flattered that I've been reached out to by so many gay fans. I think it's funny. If barriers were broken down at my expense, I'm happy about it.

CAME OFF AS:

A really weird dude. I think viewers are pretty stumped by me. But I think they respect me. At least I was honest.

SHOCKER:

That argument with Janet when I run out wearing my tight underwear. I was so drunk. When I saw it, I was shocked. I didn't even know it had happened. I was screaming at the television set, "Dude, you're in your underwear! What are you thinking?" At least I was wearing my Joe Boxers. They make my legs look good.

TOTAL CRINGE:

That whole Aubie confrontation. I hated having to confront her, and I hated watching it.

When I got back home after doing *The Real World*, I was on this huge high. Oh my God, what I just lived through! I felt like such a champ. But then I really came down. Where are the people? Where are the cameras? Getting over *The Real World* is a whole other "process." I got home, and I was so happy to be with my family. But the show—I can't deny it, you get a lot of attention, and I missed that. But of course, I had a lot to deal with. When I left *The Real World,* that's when I really had to deal with the loss of Bill, my best friend.

Janet alludes to it on the show, but I was getting terrible migraines. I can get really stressed. Losing somebody brings out all these insecurities. I was feeling unsure of everything, that life could be taken away so quickly. It was a hard

LINDSAY AND HER MOM

I wanted to deal with other stuff. I've got tons to do. I want to graduate on time, which means I had to take full course loads to compensate for last year. I really wanted to be out of college. I wanted to start life.

I was a film major. The only thing I watched on TV was the news. If I was watching anything else, it was for my film class. I took one class, a TV class, that dealt with ethical issues and the media. It definitely illuminated my experience on *The Real World*. Reality-based TV was on the syllabus. We actually studied the Stephen and Irene slap. I gave a small lecture to that class—and to my documentary class as well.

One reason I don't watch the shows so intently is that I don't like to look at myself. It's very weird to see yourself on TV. You're your own worst critic.

IF MY FAMILY HAS A CREDO, IT'S THIS: YOU DO WHAT YOU DO, YOU REFLECT AND LEARN AND THEN YOU MOVE ON. AFTER THE SHOW WAS OVER, AND I SPENT TIME WITH MY FAMILY, AND SCHOOL STARTED AGAIN, THAT'S WHAT I DID: I MOVED ON. I WANTED TO PUT EVERYTHING BEHIND ME. I DIDN'T WANT TO DWELL ON THE PAST. I WANTED TO GET ON WITH MY LIFE.

period of grieving. During that time, I spoke to Janet and Stephanie a lot. You don't see it on the show, but Stephanie and I actually got really close.

I didn't even really watch the show. I know it sounds unbelievable, but it's true. When we'd get the tapes in the mail, I'd just fast-forward through them. It's not that I wasn't interested. It's just that I wanted to preserve my own memories of my time there. I wanted to remember my life as it was. And

And it doesn't feel so hot when I meet people on the street and they tell me I look a lot better in person. I'm like, "Okay, thanks, I must have gained twenty-five pounds!" When you're on camera all the time, you have to worry: "S**t, it's not just my boyfriend that's seeing me get fat, it's everyone."

I love doing the stuff, but I don't like the reviewing or analyzing part. I know that sounds weird, since I want to do broadcasting for a living. The

CAME OFF AS:

Hyper and all over the place in the beginning and intense at the end.

FAVORITE MOMENT:

When my brother and Bill came and we took that fishing trip. You only see a second of it, but I was having the best time.

LEAST FAVORITE MOMENT:

Finding out about Bill. I actually watched that one twice before it aired. That's because I was shooting a public service announcement to be seen after the show, and I wanted to fully understand it.

DIRTY LAUNDRY:

I can still conjure up David's horrible smell, if I have to. All I need to do is think about it, and I get a whiff.

SPEED DIAL:

Janet, I haven't seen that much. We speak some. When we get to talk, it's great. I'd like to talk to her more. Same with David, Nathan, and Stephen. Rebecca, I haven't seen or talked to. Irene, I hope she's doing well, but I don't know if I'll ever speak to her again. Knowing how bad I am at calling people, I probably won't. I haven't see her on the lecture circuit, but from what I hear, she looks great.

truth is: I was on *The Real World,* but I wasn't on it that much. It's my own fault. It's because I didn't open up, because I kept so much stuff from the directors and producers and cast. Looking back on it, I wish I'd been more open—most particularly about my relationship with my boyfriend, Alex. I was so in love with him. I'm still very much in love with him. He goes to school across the country, so we're in different faraway cities, but I can't get over him. He doesn't watch the show either.

Everyone on that show—cast and crew included—wanted more openness from me. I wouldn't give it. I don't function well with pressure. I just didn't care about arguing. I guarantee if once a week I'd been able to go home and decompress, I could have come back refreshed and revitalized and drummed up some emotion. But there was no downtime. From what I've seen, I think Janet came off the best. Actually, coming off the best is not the

issue. It's coming off the most as yourself, being as genuine and authentic as possible. I am too controlled and rational for that.

My friends at school don't really care about my *Real World* status. They're too busy with their own stuff, being pre-med and pre-law. Don't get me wrong, they'll take some of the perks. There's a lot of free stuff offered to you when you've been on the show. Free drinks and free dinners and tickets to things. I've gotten bumped up to

MOST HOW—IT—WAS:
I guess our jobs at the radio station.

LEAST HOW—IT—WAS:
Irene's illness. She was actually sick for a long time.

first class on airplanes and had stewardesses hand me barf bags full of little alcohol bottles.

Perks aside, it's been significantly harder to date since *The Real World*. All the *Real World* guys are like, "woo hoo!" Chicks just come up to them and tell them they think they're hot. It's not like that for me. No one cares or seems to care, and anyway, would that matter? I'd rather I actually clicked with someone. Probably the most exciting thing about being a cast member is becoming part of the *Real World* family. I've met Heather B., whom I love, and Jason. He's a really laid-back guy. I would have liked to see things work for him and Janet.

It's amazing to be part of this show. It's a big marker for Generation X. I know the concept of *The Real World* will be always be remembered, but in a decade, will we? I don't think so. But that's okay.

THE VIEW:
I was asked to be a co-host candidate on *The View*. It was such an honor. Barbara Walters is my idol. It was really a positive experience—even though I knew I was too young to get the job. I mean, I'm still in college. I don't know what it's like to pay my own bills. But it was a great experience. And there were touches of glamour. I was flown to New York. Ms. Walters let me use her car and driver. I was in an elevator and Connie Chung walked in; and I got to meet Eriq La Salle and Richard Simmons.

On the unglamorous side, I had to do a workout segment. I'd put on five pounds and my stomach was a little gooey. The night before, I did a hundred sit-ups. I was completely sore the next day.

FAME:
People approach me pretty often. It's annoying when I'm hung over or cranky, but usually it's pretty funny and nice. Usually people ask me how the hell I keep my hair like I do. Or they ask me if Stephen is gay. I'm like, I don't know, what do *you* think?

One of the best things is that people come up to me a lot and tell me about their losses. It's really incredible that people can be so honest, and I think the show inspires that. I'm glad they feel they can talk to me.

TOTAL CRINGE:
Honestly, all the interview footage makes me cringe. All the interviews—seeing your face that big. It's not necessary. Whenever I came to my face, I had to turn away. I must have put on some weight or I'm freckled as hell.

FASHION FLUB:
Oh my God, how can I regret wearing a certain outfit, when I wore the same thing every day? All black!

FAMILY FLAK:
My mom saw the first one. Then she stopped watching, because I was never on it. My brother, he's seen the show, but he's not a religious watcher by any means. He has so much going on. We'd like to live with each other next year.

THE AFTERWORD

How to Be an Ex-*Real World*-er who goes on *The Real World/Road Rules Challenge* or Abstractions on the Last Day of the Trip

BY NEIL, THE REAL WORLD-LONDON

there's something whining under my bed.

i half wake from a dream where trent reznor is being chased by a pack of baying hounds. there's a slight twinge in my left prefrontal cortex and a dull throb at my temples. my fingers smell of reconstituted meat products and deep fried monosodium glutamate. somewhere in the distance, johnny cash is singing.

where the hell am i?

i open my eyes to an unblinking cyclops. no... i focus, it's a tv camera, and for whatever reason, its presence seems quite normal. struggling to find some meaning, i remember something of psychopath psychology. it's all about extroversion and low inhibition.

around me are the tired twisted bodies of my traveling companions—a handpicked ensemble of crowd pleasers, a mismatch of pre-millennium punk, perv approxima and pop rocks, on a corporate-funded mission across kalifornia. we are bright and beautiful.

welcome to the world of mtv, have a nice day
i start conjugating verbs in my head, tweak, position, manipulate, all in the past perfect tense. it calms me enough that i'm able to drag myself from the heart of the carnage. i realize i'm in a bed with jason and janet. the bed is round and there are mirrors on the walls and ceiling. the sign above the door says 'this is not an exit.'

i stumble over bodies and debris, as i step out into the searing heat of a beverly hills morning. it's hot here, most unnatural. i'm in real danger of losing my pale blue complexion. my skin is burnt and blistered. the varnish on my nails is chipped and claggy. glamour always seems to fade with the first rays of the morning sun.

i'm past ripe, it seems. i'm rotting.

a vague memory of anne and a trampoline makes my foot twinge, but no matter, i'm off to los angeles to blow up bessie, the winnebago. it seems a fitting conclusion. i put on the blackest of black cotton t-shirts and my cat-eyed sunglasses, the darkest in my collection. all for bessie.

this is the last day and i'm on my way home. i'm stiff and sweaty, I still have mud between my teeth after yesterdays unfortunate encounter with the military. in twenty four hours i've gone from high explosives to high pneumatics, i've seen the twin pinnacles of the american dream, a multimillion dollar house built on the profits of pornography and the (un)questionable might of military muscle. breakfast is on the road as usual. taco bell this time, i think, they blend into one. i've never eaten so much junk food in my life. every stop is carl jr's or denny's, every other turn brings the vista of a vast open road ripping through the desert like a scar, and every twenty miles there's gas-food-lodging. i'm slick with the grease of a thousand drive-thrus. i've been on the road for two weeks and it seems like a year.

i know that by the time this gets to the tv screen it'll be bite-sized and easy to digest. mindlessly consumed between hearty slices of marilyn manson's lily-white arse and peeks down madonna's metal brassiere.

i dig that.

i've grown to love this winnebago, this heap of rolling junk, she's packed full of memories and here i am waiting on the end of a wire ready to push the button that'll reduce her to a rain of smok-

ing debris. on cue, i flick my switch, and sure enough, just like in the movies, a giant fireball erupts and knocks me backwards. a single belch of acrid black smoke and she's gone. i wonder to myself what it's going to look like on tv.

i think it's over. but i'm wrong. there's still the handsome reward. i'm at a hollywood studio theme park. there are fat sweating tourists with cameras and a gaggle of squealing fans. the horror becomes apparent. i'm going to have to climb inside a plastic garbage can and grab for those dead presidents like an idiotic performing monkey in a cage. being english, dollars all look the same to me, monopoly money, and the gravity of just how much cash is flying around in this machine is completely lost on me. still, i frenziedly stuff twenties into my nice new eastpak backpack, in a protective bubble of mtv world where every day is like saturday and all the drinks are free.

i'm scarred, i'm mesmerized. i'm strangely aroused.

the tourists amble past and remark idly to each other that it must be

'some sort of mtv thing.'

How to get on

The Real World

Dear Readers:

Here's an application to be on The Real World. We're hoping that if you're interested in being on the show (and you appear to be between the ages 18 and 24), you'll fill it out. Be honest, and sincere, and tell us what issues are of interest to you. Show us why you should be on The Real World.

And to the readers who are not interested in being on the show: Why not fill it out anyway? It'll give you insight into the casting process—after all, all previous cast members had to fill this out. And, hey, you might learn something....

Good luck!

Mary-Ellis Bunim and Jonathan Murray

How can you do this? Read on for step-by-step directions.

CALL THE REAL WORLD HOTLINE: (818) 754-5790 OR CHECK OUT THE BUNIM/MURRAY PRODUCTIONS WEBSITE AT WWW.BUNIM-MURRAY.COM

This number will give you the latest information on applying, the deadlines for next season, and where to send your application.

WRITE A COVER LETTER.

We want you to tell us a little bit about yourself. Why do you want to spend six months in a house full of strangers? What activities will you pursue? Please include a snapshot of yourself in this cover letter.

MAKE A VIDEOTAPE.

We'd also like to see you as well as hear from you. Make a ten-minute videotape of yourself talking about whatever you think makes you a good candidate for *The Real World.* Remember, we want to see if you are a person who is open and willing to express what's important to you.

Sometimes, the best videos are simple—like someone sitting on their bed talking about what makes them tick. Just be honest and sincere. And don't overthink it. (Also, make sure there's enough light on your face and that you're close enough to the microphone to be heard.)

FILL OUT THE ENCLOSED APPLICATION.

Answer all the following questions as honestly as you can. Please keep your answers to a paragraph in length. And please be sure to type your answers or write legibly.

NAME:

PHONE:

SOCIAL SECURITY NO.:

PARENTS' NAMES:

DATE RECEIVED:

ADDRESS:

E-MAIL ADDRESS:

ADDRESS: PHONE: E-MAIL ADDRESS:

SIBLINGS (NAMES AND AGES):

RACE (OPTIONAL: FOR STATISTICAL PURPOSES ONLY):

HAVE YOU EVER ACTED OR PERFORMED OUTSIDE OF SCHOOL?

EDUCATION: NAME OF HIGH SCHOOL: YEARS COMPLETED:

NAME OF COLLEGE: YEARS COMPLETED AND MAJORS:

OTHER EDUCATION:

WHERE DO YOU WORK? DESCRIBE YOUR JOB HISTORY:

WHAT IS YOUR ULTIMATE CAREER GOAL?

WHAT ARE YOUR PERSONAL (NOT CAREER) GOALS IN LIFE?

WHAT KIND OF PRESSURE DO YOU FEEL ABOUT MAKING DECISIONS ABOUT YOUR FUTURE? WHO'S PUTTING THE PRESSURE ON YOU?

WHO ARE YOUR HEROES AND WHY?

WHAT ABOUT YOU WILL MAKE YOU AN INTERESTING ROOMMATE?

IF YOU'RE LIVING WITH A ROOMMATE, HOW DID YOU HOOK UP WITH HIM OR HER? TELL US ABOUT HIM OR HER AS A PERSON.
DO YOU GET ALONG? WHAT'S THE BEST PART ABOUT LIVING WITH HIM OR HER? WHAT'S THE HARDEST PART ABOUT IT?

HOW WOULD SOMEONE WHO REALLY KNOWS YOU DESCRIBE YOUR BEST TRAITS?

THE REAL WORLD APPLICATION FORM

HOW WOULD SOMEONE WHO REALLY KNOWS YOU DESCRIBE YOUR WORST TRAITS?

DESCRIBE YOUR MOST EMBARRASSING MOMENT IN LIFE:

DO YOU HAVE A BOYFRIEND OR GIRLFRIEND? HOW LONG HAVE YOU TWO BEEN TOGETHER? WHERE DO YOU SEE THE RELATIONSHIP GOING? WHAT DRIVES YOU CRAZY ABOUT THE OTHER PERSON? WHAT'S THE BEST THING ABOUT THE OTHER PERSON?

HOW IMPORTANT IS SEX TO YOU? DO YOU HAVE IT ONLY WHEN YOU'RE IN A RELATIONSHIP OR DO YOU SEEK IT OUT AT OTHER TIMES? HOW DID IT COME ABOUT ON THE LAST OCCASION?

DESCRIBE YOUR FANTASY DATE:

WHAT QUALITIES DO YOU SEEK IN A MATE?

WHAT ARTISTIC TALENTS DO YOU HAVE (MUSIC, ART, DANCE, PERFORMANCE, FILM/VIDEO MAKING, WRITING, ETC.)? HOW SKILLED ARE YOU?

DO YOU LIKE TRAVELLING? DESCRIBE ONE OR TWO OF THE BEST OR WORST TRIPS YOU HAVE TAKEN. WHERE WOULD YOU MOST LIKE TO TRAVEL?

WHAT DO YOU DO FOR FUN?

DO YOU PLAY ANY SPORTS?

WHAT ARE YOUR FAVORITE MUSICAL GROUPS/ARTISTS?

DESCRIBE A TYPICAL FRIDAY OR SATURDAY NIGHT:

WHAT WAS THE LAST UNUSUAL, EXCITING, OR SPONTANEOUS OUTING YOU INSTIGATED FOR YOU AND YOUR FRIENDS?

OTHER THAN A BOYFRIEND OR GIRLFRIEND, WHO IS THE MOST IMPORTANT PERSON IN YOUR LIFE RIGHT NOW? TELL US ABOUT HIM OR HER:

WHAT ARE SOME WAYS YOU HAVE TREATED SOMEONE WHO HAS BEEN IMPORTANT TO YOU THAT YOU ARE PROUD OF?

WHAT ARE SOME OF THE WAYS YOU HAVE TREATED SOMEONE WHO HAS BEEN IMPORTANT TO YOU THAT YOU ARE EMBARRASSED BY, OR WISH YOU HADN'T DONE?

IF YOU HAD TO DESCRIBE YOUR MOTHER (OR YOUR STEPMOTHER, IF YOU LIVED WITH HER MOST OF YOUR LIFE AS A CHILD), BY DIVIDING HER PERSONALITY INTO TWO PARTS, HOW WOULD YOU DESCRIBE EACH PART?

IF YOU HAD TO DESCRIBE YOUR FATHER (OR YOUR STEPFATHER), BY DIVIDING HIS PERSONALITY INTO TWO PARTS, HOW WOULD YOU DESCRIBE EACH PART?

HOW DID YOUR PARENTS TREAT EACH OTHER? DID YOUR PARENTS HAVE A GOOD MARRIAGE? WHAT WAS IT LIKE?

DESCRIBE HOW CONFLICTS WERE HANDLED AT HOME AS YOU WERE GROWING UP (WHO WOULD WIN AND WHO WOULD LOSE, WHETHER THERE WAS YELLING OR HITTING, ETC.)?

IF YOU HAVE ANY BROTHERS OR SISTERS, ARE YOU CLOSE? HOW WOULD YOU DESCRIBE YOUR RELATIONSHIP WITH THEM?

DESCRIBE A MAJOR EVENT OR ISSUE THAT'S AFFECTED YOUR FAMILY:

DESCRIBE A QUALITY/TRAIT THAT RUNS IN YOUR FAMILY:

WHAT IS THE MOST IMPORTANT ISSUE OR PROBLEM FACING YOU TODAY?

IS THERE ANY ISSUE, POLITICAL OR SOCIAL, THAT YOU'RE PASSIONATE ABOUT? HAVE YOU DONE ANYTHING ABOUT IT?

DO YOU BELIEVE IN GOD? ARE YOU RELIGIOUS OR SPIRITUAL? DO YOU ATTEND ANY FORMAL RELIGIOUS SERVICES?

WHAT ARE YOUR THOUGHTS ON: ABORTION?

OTHER SEXUAL ORIENTATIONS?

WELFARE?

AFFIRMATIVE ACTION?

DO YOU HAVE ANY HABITS WE SHOULD KNOW ABOUT?

DO YOU: SMOKE CIGARETTES?

DRINK ALCOHOL? HOW OLD WERE YOU WHEN YOU HAD YOUR FIRST DRINK? HOW MUCH DO YOU DRINK NOW? HOW OFTEN?

DO YOU USE RECREATIONAL DRUGS? WHAT DRUGS HAVE YOU USED? HOW OFTEN?

_____

THE REAL WORLD AND *ROAD RULES* HAVE A ZERO TOLERANCE DRUG POLICY. IF YOU USE DRUGS, CAN YOU GO WITHOUT FOR SEVERAL MONTHS?

DO YOU KNOW A LOT OF PEOPLE WHO DO DRUGS? WHAT DO YOU THINK OF PEOPLE WHO DO DRUGS?

_____

ARE YOU ON ANY PRESCRIPTION MEDICATION? IF SO, WHAT, AND FOR HOW LONG HAVE YOU BEEN TAKING IT?

_____

HAVE YOU EVER BEEN ARRESTED? (IF SO, WHAT WAS THE CHARGE AND WERE YOU CONVICTED?)

_____

WHAT BOTHERS YOU MOST ABOUT OTHER PEOPLE?

_____

DESCRIBE A RECENT MAJOR ARGUMENT YOU HAD WITH SOMEONE. WHO USUALLY WINS ARGUMENTS WITH YOU? WHY?

_____

_____

HAVE YOU EVER HIT ANYONE IN ANGER OR SELF-DEFENSE? IF SO, TELL US ABOUT IT (HOW OLD WERE YOU, WHAT HAPPENED, ETC.)

_____

IF YOU COULD CHANGE ONE THING ABOUT THE WAY YOU LOOK, WHAT WOULD THAT BE?

_____

IF YOU COULD CHANGE ONE THING ABOUT YOUR PERSONALITY, WHAT WOULD THAT BE?

IF SELECTED, IS THERE ANY PERSON OR PART OF YOUR LIFE YOU WOULD PREFER NOT TO SHARE? IF SO, DESCRIBE
(I.E. FAMILY, FRIENDS, BUSINESS ASSOCIATES, SOCIAL ORGANIZATIONS, OR ACTIVITIES)

_____

IS THERE ANYONE AMONG YOUR FAMILY OR CLOSE FRIENDS WHO WOULD OBJECT TO APPEARING ON CAMERA? IF SO, WHY?

_____

ARE YOU NOW SEEING, OR HAVE YOU EVER SEEN, A THERAPIST OR PSYCHOLOGIST?

WHAT IS YOUR GREATEST FEAR (AND WHY)?

_____

IF YOU HAD ALADDIN'S LAMP AND THREE WISHES, WHAT WOULD THEY BE?

_____

PLEASE RATE THE FOLLOWING ACTIVITIES/PASTTIMES USING THE FOLLOWING SCALE: N: NEVER   S: SOMETIMES   O: OFTEN   A: ALWAYS

	RATING	COMMENT
READ BOOKS		
SLEEP 8 HOURS		
WATCH TELEVISION DAILY		
SHOP		
GO OUT/SOCIALIZE		
SPEND TIME WITH FRIENDS		

	RATING	COMMENT
SPEND TIME ALONE		
WORK/STUDY		
TALK ON THE PHONE		
COOK		
CLEAN		
ARGUE		
WRITE		
READ NEWSPAPERS		
ENJOY THE COMPANY OF ANIMALS		
STATE OPINIONS		
ASK OPINIONS		
CONFIDE IN YOUR PARENTS		
VOLUNTEER		
PROCRASTINATE		
EAT		
DRINK ALCOHOL		
DIET		
SMOKE		
CRY		
LAUGH		
MOVIES		
THEATRE		
CLUBS		
PARTIES		

THE REAL WORLD APPLICATION FORM

LIST 4 PEOPLE WHO HAVE KNOWN YOU FOR A LONG TIME (EXCLUDING RELATIVES) AND WILL TELL US WHAT A GREAT PERSON YOU ARE: (PLEASE INCLUDE TWO ADULTS AND TWO OF YOUR FRIENDS).

1. NAME ___ ADDRESS ___ PHONE ___ HOW DO THEY KNOW YOU?

2. NAME ___ ADDRESS ___ PHONE ___ HOW DO THEY KNOW YOU?

3. NAME ___ ADDRESS ___ PHONE ___ HOW DO THEY KNOW YOU?

4. NAME ___ ADDRESS ___ PHONE ___ HOW DO THEY KNOW YOU?

HOW DID YOU HEAR ABOUT OUR CASTING SEARCH?

SIGNATURE ___ DATE ___

Thank you for your time and effort in completing this form.